HOW ZOE MADE HER DREAMS (MOSTLY) COME TRUE

Also by Sarah Strohmeyer

Smart Girls Get What They Want

HOW ZOE MADE HER DREAMS (MOSTLY) COME TRUE

by SARAH STROHMEYER

BALZER + BRAY
An Imprint of HarperCollins*Publishers*

Balzer + Bray is an imprint of HarperCollins Publishers.

How Zoe Made Her Dreams (Mostly) Come True
Copyright © 2013 by Sarah Strohmeyer
All rights reserved. Printed in the United States of America.
No part of this book may be used or reproduced in any manner whatsoever without written permission except in the case of brief quotations embodied in critical articles and reviews. For information address HarperCollins Children's Books, a division of HarperCollins Publishers, 10 East 53rd Street, New York, NY 10022.
www.epicreads.com

Library of Congress Cataloging-in-Publication Data
Strohmeyer, Sarah.
How Zoe made her dreams (mostly) come true / Sarah Strohmeyer. — 1st ed.
p.   cm.
Summary: Seventeen-year-old Zoe and her cousin Jess eagerly start summer jobs at New Jersey's Fairyland theme park, but Jess does not get her dream role and Zoe is assigned to be personal assistant to the park's "Queen," winning her no friends.
ISBN 978-0-06-218745-1 (pbk. bdg.)
[1. Amusement parks—Fiction.   2. Summer employment—Fiction.
3. Cousins—Fiction.   4. New Jersey—Fiction.]   I. Title.
PZ7.S52152How 2013   2012038163
[Fic]—dc23

Typography by Michelle Gengaro-Kokmen
13 14 15 16 17 LP/RRDH 10 9 8 7 6 5 4 3 2 1
❖

First Edition

To the ever youthful Randy Reynolds Briggs.
May you get (almost) everything you want.

Prologue

There was no getting around the fact that Tinker Bell was a little bitch.

The tiny, white powder-puff bichon frise with professionally manicured toenails scampered under the thornbush and out of sight. Aghast, I stared at her diamond-studded collar swinging perilously from her leash like a noose swaying from the gallows. It was way after curfew. We were deep in the forest, and my evil boss's perfumed purse ornament had just taken off after an imaginary squirrel.

"Tink!" I hissed, trying to catch glimpses of white in the murky undergrowth. "Come back here, you spoiled-rotten little Q-tip. You're going to get me fired!"

I was so tired, I could barely keep my eyes open, having been up since dawn to walk the dog and then in the Fairyland salon by six thirty, dressed in my silver gown and ready to start my day. Trish the stylist had twisted my long, brown hair into a tight updo topped with a delicate pearl headpiece; after which Helga had lined my green eyes in purple and my less-than-pouty lips in glossy pink.

At 7:02 I delivered to my boss, aka "the Queen," her usual breakfast of three raw almonds, two grapefruit slices cut into thirty pieces, one hard-boiled egg (miraculously yolk-free), a pot of Earl Grey tea with precisely two drops of honey, and the morning's newspapers—edited to remove all references to the Mouse—before sorting through her mail, reading the customer-feedback forms in what we in the Fairyland front office jokingly referred to as the Box of Whine, polishing her Magic Mirror, sorting her pencils according to length, and feeding Tinker Bell two spoonfuls of Russian caviar.

At ten I had to raid the kitchen to steal several bright red apples, since Snow White's poisoned ones were all rotten. At noon I was called to the Haunted Forest, where Hansel and Gretel (aka Brendan Borowitz and Stella McPherson) had been caught making out behind the Candy Cottage. ("Gretel was applying mouth-to-mouth resuscitation to save her brother after the witch had tried to kill him. Isn't that touching?" I told the traumatized children, pale from witnessing their first pseudoincestuous atrocity.)

Mac Weintraub as Jack took a post-lunch snooze and accidentally rolled off the beanstalk around two. I had to check if anything was broken before I called the insurance company. Oh, and did I mention Miranda Clark? She was playing Rapunzel when the air-conditioning broke in her hot, cramped tower, and she fainted. Fortunately I'd thought to bring along some spirit of hartshorn to revive her, along with serious contraband, an ice-cold can of Red Bull.

"You're a lifesaver, Zoe," Rapunzel whispered, popping it open and guzzling it in one swallow.

Not a lifesaver, actually, more like a psychic lady-in-waiting working behind the scenes to save my fellow Fairyland cohorts from imminent disaster while trying to anticipate my boss's every whim. Though, at midnight, maybe not so much.

The iPhone in my pocket trilled the strains of "Every Breath You Take" right as Tink's furry butt slipped out of my hands. "Where are you, Zoe?" Her Majesty inquired in her nasal voice. "I want to go to bed, and I need my Tinksy Winksy." There was an ominous pause. "I hope you haven't lost her."

I shivered at the veiled threat in her icy tone. "No, ma'am." *Not yet.* "Tinksy wants to stay out longer."

The Queen yawned. "Very well, then. I'll wait up."

Oh, please don't, I thought as she hung up. "Tink. Where are you? Come back here!"

We weren't supposed to leave the park perimeter. It was strictly forbidden. Did I dare go farther?

Either that, or lose the dog.

Right. I did not want to think of the punishment that would await me if I returned to the palace without Tinker Bell.

Summoning my courage and keeping my ears cocked for the pitter-patter of tiny, manicured doggy toes, I padded across the soft forest floor, ignoring the distinct feeling that several sets of eyes were upon me. Owls, perhaps. Night creatures. Carnivorous plants. Security patrols. With only the bright moon overhead for light, I negotiated fallen trees and rotting logs, and the occasional nasty root and pricker bush, until I almost smacked into something hard. A wall.

It wasn't Fairyland's outside wall. That was lit from above, its granite stones regularly polished to a brilliant, toothy whiteness. This wall was dark and mossy. This wall was old.

I was running my hands over the dips and valleys, trying to figure out where I could be, when all of a sudden my right foot went through the ground and I was up to my hip in cold, damp sand.

"Crap!"

Profanity was prohibited in Fairyland, but it wasn't like anyone was there to bust me. I was trapped in a sink-hole, alone in the forest, and worst of all, Tinker Bell was long gone. I tried pushing myself out and found, much to my dismay, that the more pressure I applied, the more the ground gave way.

There was another rustle in the bushes. *Tinker Bell?* If I could nab the dog, that'd be half the battle. The two of us could huddle in the hole until morning, when the Queen sent someone to find her precious baby.

"Tink?" I called, stretching out my hand, hopeful for the wet nose, the rough lick of her tiny, pink tongue. *"I have caviar!"*

The rustling got closer and louder. My heart started to beat harder. This was no bichon frise. This was a much larger animal—like a human.

I detected a whiff of cologne that only the Prince Charmings were allowed to wear, spicy and so aromatic, it made you swoon. Then I heard someone say, "Gotcha!" and I was eye-to-eye with a pair of hiking boots. I looked up, but all I could see was a ball of white wriggling in some boy's arms.

"Seems as though you've dug yourself into quite a hole there, Zoe," he said, sounding amused.

Not for the first time did I curse the fact that, like the

princesses, all the Prince Charmings had been taught to speak in "the Queen's English"—complete with upper-crust British pronunciation—so visitors wouldn't be able to distinguish one from another. He could have been any one of eight hot guys, and it didn't help that his face was shadowed by the moonlight above.

I said, "I'm stuck. Can you give me a hand up?"

"I could," he taunted. "But then, as the Queen's lady-in-waiting, you'd report me for being outside the park after curfew, and I would be fired and . . ."

"No, I won't." Honestly, I'd never do such a thing. "I will be forever in your debt."

"Really?"

"Really."

"Forever in my debt, you say?"

"Yes." *Please just get me out of here.*

"I'll hold you to that, you know. So when I come to collect, you can't back out and claim the *whole* thing never happened. Or that it was all a *whole* big mistake."

"Fine. Whatever." Here I was, slipping deeper into this pit, and he was making puns. Typical cocky prince.

Tinker Bell emitted a mewling sound of annoyance.

"All right. Hold on." He placed Tinker Bell in my arms. "But we'll have to do it the right way. Wait here." He gave another laugh and trudged off, returning minutes later with a long branch. "I'm going to stand clear of the sinkhole so I don't fall in, which won't do either of us any good. You hold tight and try to claw your way out."

It seemed like an impossibly tall order, clutching Tink and a branch while extricating myself from what essentially amounted to quicksand, but I did my best, scrabbling and clawing as Tink kicked in protest. At last we were free. I stumbled to where he'd been standing and leaned against a tree, breathing hard.

"Thank you!" I said.

No sound.

"Hello?"

He was gone, except for a sizable swatch of black flannel dangling from a thornbush. I picked it off and held it to my nose, inhaling the unique scent of the Prince Charming cologne. Yes, definitely his.

Stuffing the torn piece of shirt into my back pocket, I found my way to the path and ran as fast as I could, Her Majesty's royal fluff ball bouncing in my arms. Had this been a *real* fairyland and I had been a *real* lady-in-waiting to a *real* evil queen, perhaps a pumpkin carriage or a knight on horseback might have come to my rescue.

But this wasn't a real fairyland. It was Fairyland Kingdom, a destination fairy-tale theme park in the Pinelands of southern New Jersey, and I was a seventeen-year-old cast member interning for the summer in an exclusive program that thousands of teenagers from across the world auditioned for every year. I was lucky to be here—*everyone said so*—even though I was fast learning that behind the sweetly smiling princesses and dashing princes, there was a secret world that wasn't oh-so-innocent.

That night, I showered off the sand and slid under my own sheets, slipping the prince's shirt swatch beneath my pillow for safekeeping. Home at last.

As I drifted off to blissful sleep, I tried to recall my rosy expectations when Jess and I had arrived at Fairyland only a few weeks before, how we'd looked forward to a pleasant summer of dressing up in costumes and entertaining children, while in our off-hours getting to know the extremely cute princes.

Oh, how wrong I'd been. Fairyland was nothing like I'd imagined, except maybe for the princes.

They were even better.

One

The day after we finished our junior year at Bridgewater-Raritan High, Jess and I hopped into her dad's 1998 Honda Bobmobile and hightailed it down the Garden State to Fairyland with the windows open and our hair flying, Springsteen blaring at full volume. Personally I'm not a big fan of the Boss, but I'm pretty sure it's a state law that if you're on a road trip in Jersey, "Thunder Road" is de rigueur—even at 6:00 a.m.

I know, crazy. Who gets up that early the first free day of summer? Fairyland interns, that's who. Everyone had to be at the park by eight. It said so in the thick, sparkly welcome packet we'd received along with the official letter congratulating us on being selected as Fairyland

Kingdom Inc. summer cast members from thousands of rising high school seniors.

I still couldn't get over that we'd been accepted or, rather, that *I* had, since Jess had been acting since she was a kid, so she deserved an internship. Me? I'm a disaster on stage, going left when everyone else is going right, forgetting lines, and, in the case of my debut as an ant in our second-grade performance of *Aesop's Fables*, projectile vomiting.

In fact, I was so convinced my acceptance had been some sort of clerical error that I was prepared to be rejected as soon as we arrived. This was why I'd made Jess borrow her dad's car, so I could drive it home after the inevitable.

"Stop putting yourself down. You kicked butt in the auditions," Jess said, gripping the wheel at two and ten like a little old lady, her seat pushed all the way forward so her short legs could reach the gas pedal. God forbid we should get in a fender bender because, if the airbag deployed, she'd have been shot straight through the rear.

"You should sit back more, or your head's going to pop off in an accident," I said, applying the last strip of purple shellac to my pinkie toe that was propped on the dashboard.

"If I sit back, I can't see over the wheel."

Jess is petite like that. Tiny nose. Childlike fingers.

Wispy, pale blond hair that she usually yanks into a ponytail so it doesn't fly into her clear blue eyes. All her life people have been telling her she's a little Cinderella, sweet and kind. (Yeah, right. They haven't seen her spike a volleyball with seconds on the clock.) Often these same people find it kind of hard to believe that we're cousins.

"Really?" I remember our neighbor Mrs. Coughlin exclaiming, when she'd learned Jess and I were related. "But you're so different, Zoe." Meaning, I suppose, that I was tall with brown hair and green eyes and not so delicate, since I liked to noogie her son, Curtis, on whom I had a huge crush.

"That's why we're best friends!" Jess had piped up in her cheerful way. "Because we're opposites!"

I was so relieved we both got internships. Can you imagine how awkward it would have been if I got in and not Jess, or vice versa? I didn't even want to think about it, and we weren't out of the woods yet, since we hadn't received our cast assignments. That was fine by me, but for a variety of reasons, some practical, Jess had her heart set on being a princess.

If they made her Elf #6 or any of the "lesser" characters like Goldilocks or, *shudder*, a furry, for which she'd have to wear a hot bear or wolf costume and run around in ninety-degree heat, she'd be crushed. At her size, almost literally.

We got off at exit 52, and as soon as we took a right, there were the purple turrets of the Princess Palace flying banana yellow flags with the Cow Jumped Over the Moon roller coaster behind it. Jess and I squealed like we used to when we were little kids and her mom, Aunt Nancy, and mine—twin sisters—would take us for the whole day. Our families were too broke to afford a week at the shore, so Fairyland was the highlight of summer vacation, and Mom spared no expense. She bought us crowns and fairy wings and pink tutus that we held out to curtsy when Cinderella or Sleeping Beauty passed by with one of their Prince Charmings.

I shouldn't have let myself think about those sparkly, blue-sky days that smelled of coconut sunblock and popcorn that would never, ever be again, because I immediately plummeted into one of my funks. Jess, catching me fingering the single-pearl necklace that used to be Mom's, shifted the Bobmobile into park and said, "You okay?"

I said, "Uh-huh. I'm fine."

But Jess knew. She'd been there with me from the beginning, when Mom came clean about the diagnosis after admirably trying to pass off her nausea and exhaustion as stress. It was Jess who'd looked up all the reassuring survivor stories online and showed up on my doorstep with bags of barbecue potato chips, ice cream, chocolate sauce, M&Ms, those chemically questionable maraschino cherries, and whipped cream, plus *Ferris Bueller's Day Off* and *Legally Blonde* (1 & 2) to keep me distracted.

Jess had stuck with me to the bitter end—unlike Derek James, the crappiest boyfriend ever, who didn't break up with me before the funeral only because his parents insisted that would have been cruel. Or so his subsequent girlfriend, Zara Cavalerie, couldn't wait to tell me.

Meanwhile, I had been so caught up in the day-to-day slog of sickness and losing Mom and generally feeling sorry for myself that I hadn't noticed that Jess's family was falling apart, too. Not healthwise, thank god, but, rather, financially. One day her parents were gainfully employed at the local pharmaceutical company; the next thing I knew they'd been out of work for six months, and Jess was getting nervous.

Not that she complained—that's the thing about Jess: she hardly ever does—but all of a sudden she couldn't go shopping, and a trip to the movies was too expensive when, before, we didn't think twice. She even had a job scooping Häagen-Dazs at the mall and still didn't have a penny to spare. It was weird, and when I'd finally asked her what was up, she'd admitted that she was handing her paychecks to her parents, who'd already blown through her college fund.

I mean, there was nothing left in their savings. Not

even five bucks for a measly spiral-bound notebook. And now Jess was looking at living at home after graduation while maybe taking a course at the Raritan Valley Community College instead of going to her dream school, Tisch, for drama at NYU.

"What are the chances of me actually breaking out as an actress, anyway?" she asked as we drove to Fairyland. "My money—that is, if I had money—would be wasted. Better to be practical and learn something useful. Like accounting."

Jess could not count out change on a ten-dollar bill for a $6.79 Banana Split Dazzler down at the Dazs, so I couldn't imagine her holed up in a cubicle doing people's taxes. If she refused to have an honest discussion with her parents about money and college, because she didn't want them to feel guilty for spending her NYU tuition, then I'd take charge.

After all, Jess had saved me from falling to pieces a year and a half ago. The least I could do in return was to help her now.

Oddly enough, that's where Cinderella came in.

It came as no surprise that Fairyland Kingdom—where even the trash cans are spotless—had planned a super-organized orientation for the interns. There was a place for us to stash our car for a week, until Jess's dad came to pick it up, and a place for our luggage (two bags, max) and a special gate where we had to check in.

There a scrub-faced Keebler Elf type named Andy the Summer Cast Coordinator crossed out our names (I was on the list—relief!) and handed us matching T-shirts that said Wow!™—the rather uninspired one-word motto of Fairyland.

We pulled those on over our tops, slapped on white name tags, and proceeded to the orientation table, where we were each given a book entitled *Fairyland Kingdom Internship Handbook & Rules* and our room keys. Jess and I were thrilled that Fairyland had honored our requests and made us roomies, though we were kind of disappointed to learn we wouldn't be in one of the turrets. Those, apparently, were reserved for princes and princesses.

Jess went white.

I said, "It doesn't mean you're not a princess."

"Yes, it does." She looked like she was about to faint. I panicked.

Turning to the orientation lady who'd just given us our room keys, I said, "I'm sorry to be a pest, but can you check if Jess Swynkowski has been cast as a princess?" The woman had our files right there, so it shouldn't have been a big deal.

"You'll get your cast assignments after breakfast. We

have to keep the line moving." She waved toward a tall, dark-haired guy behind us. "Next!"

"I don't mind," he said. "I can wait."

"Rules are rules," she snapped. "And Fairyland has them for a reason, so you kids better get used to that. Now, what's your last name, son? Did you say Davidson?"

I smiled to thank him for trying. He shrugged, like he hadn't done anything.

Maybe some breakfast would help, since even as a little kid Jess had been the type to get woozy if she didn't have her beloved apples and peanut butter by recess. I led her under the white banner that said Welcome, Fairyland Kingdom Summer Interns . . . Wow!™ to a grassy slope and, suddenly, I was starving, too. Glorious breakfasty aromas of coffee, waffles, and hot chocolate wafted from a huge, white tent where lots of the summer cast were milling about in their Wow!™ T-shirts.

Let me state for the record that I have never seen so many beautiful people my own age in real life. Seriously, it was like stepping into an A&F catalog without the preppy bright green shorts. The girls were mega pretty, with long red, blond, or brunette hair conditioned to Pantene perfection. The boys were tall and slim, with sculpted muscles and perfect skin. They stood with their legs slightly apart, flipping their bangs every two seconds in a way that would have been annoying if they hadn't been so cute. I wanted to kidnap one and take him back to Bridgewater as a pet.

Jess went, "Wow."

"I know, right?" That Fairyland motto might have been less than original, but it certainly was apt.

Too bad Ari, my grief counselor, had made me promise to give up guys for a while. The way he saw it, I was still too needy and hurting from Mom's passing to be in a romantic relationship. One of his last pieces of advice before the end of school was: "Let's make this the summer when Zoe grows out of her cocoon and emerges as a fantastic butterfly."

The cocoon reference was because I'd been spending most of my days holed up in our wood-paneled TV room sipping iced soy lattes, knitting cotton washcloths, and watching a slew of reality TV shows, my favorite being *Teenage Pregnant Nightmare* with which I was completely obsessed. It wasn't the healthiest of addictions, I'll agree, but it got me over a rough patch, and on some level Karolynne and her baby daddy Hunter Boxworth provided a fascinating lesson in sociology. Anyway, I could see the value of healing before opening my heart again for love, so I'd told Ari okay.

But that was before I saw *him*.

He was thoughtfully selecting an orange to go with

his grapes and strawberries. His jeans were faded, and his tanned wrists were bedecked with various bracelets in worn, brown hemp. He obviously was into hiking or something equally granolaish, because his hair, naturally brown, was sun-streaked, and his shoes were beaten and muddy.

Have I mentioned that I'm a sucker for earthy, outdoorsy guys? That may seem ironic, considering my leanings toward the hermit lifestyle. Guess Jess was right: Opposites really do attract.

Jess followed my line of sight and said, "Hemp bracelets, Zoe. Need I say more?" She had a thing against guys who wore hemp bracelets. Also, dusters.

I grabbed a hot white china plate at the buffet. "I don't care. I'm going in."

Considering that I hadn't done anything with a guy since my funeral-era boyfriend, Derek James, I was feeling rustier than a seventh grader caked in Clearasil at her first dance. I just stood there holding my plate and trying to sneak a glance at his name tag—*Dash*. When he handed me the tongs to the fruit bowl and said, "Man, I could eat a horse," the best I could manage was a witty, "Yeah."

At that point in my suavity, I knocked a strawberry to the ground, picked it up, dusted it off, and ate it just to show I could be hard-ass that way. Dash regarded me in amusement. "You *ate* that?"

I ignored the questionable crunch of grit and swallowed. "Uh-huh. It wasn't too bad. Better than a horse."

"You know, I wouldn't really eat a horse," he said. "Seeing as how I'm a vegan."

"Hey, me too!" This wasn't exactly true when it came to chocolate, ice cream, and pizza, three of the four essential food groups, but I didn't feel like footnoting.

"Then we'll have to stick together," he said.

"One in two-fu." Inwardly I groaned.

He winced. "That was awful."

"Thank you." I bowed. "I'm here all summer." We grinned at each other, and then he said, "Bye," and I said, "See ya."

Not too bad for a shut-in, I thought, giving myself a mental pat on the back.

"Vegan, huh?" The dark-haired guy who'd been behind us in the orientation line now stood on the other side of the fruit bowl, picking out all the watermelon. The rest of his plate was filled with various meat products.

I really didn't want to get into "the vegan thing" with someone I didn't know, so I gave him my standard line. "It's a personal choice."

"I get that. I just don't know why." He studied his watermelon supply and went for a few more. "I mean, I understand vegetarianism. Don't want to kill animals. Sure. But vegan makes no sense. I can't really see the harm in milking a cow or eating eggs that won't ever grow up to be chickens."

"If you really want to know, I'll tell you," I said, trying not to get heated, because he'd been nice to me with the orientation lady and everything.

He put down the tongs. "I really want to know."

"Okay, well, for starters, the whole poultry industry is evil. Do you know how those chickens live? Cooped up in the same cage their entire lives, not getting out once. It's criminal."

He boldly bit into a sausage, not even pausing to consider how I might have been offended. "Have you ever been around chickens?"

"Have you . . ." I checked his name tag. "*Ian?*"

"My dad has 'em on his ranch in Colorado. Man, do they smell." He wrinkled his nose. "And talk about nasty personalities. They'll peck each other to death, you know. They're cannibals. Swear to god, cannibal chickens. Sounds like a Gary Larson cartoon, but it's true."

"No, it's not." Sheesh. The pro-poultry propaganda some people believe.

He took me by the arm and moved me outside, since, apparently, we were hogging the fruit table. "If we were allowed to go online here, I'd tell you to search Wikipedia for chickens plus cannibals so you could verify."

"Wikipedia's your source?" That was laughable. "Oh,

please. The poultry industry probably paid big money to get chicken cannibals on there. It's an urban myth."

He grinned and his eyes crinkled. All of a sudden he looked really familiar—the mop of black hair, the prominent jaw, the constant half smile—though I was almost positive I'd never met him before. "Why would the poultry industry spread a myth that chickens were cannibals?" he asked.

"So you wouldn't feel bad eating their eggs."

"I wouldn't feel bad eating their eggs if chickens were the sweetest things on earth. You know why?"

"Why?"

"Because they're . . . *chickens*!" He threw up an arm. "And where I'm from in Texas, chickens *are* a vegetable."

Even I, the die-hard semi-vegan, had to laugh. "I thought you were from Colorado."

"My dad's in Colorado. My mom's in Texas." Having finished his sausage, he forked a piece of watermelon while I had yet to take a bite of my own food due to certain insecurities about masticating near guys. "Long, complicated, and, ultimately, boring story."

A girl who'd been hanging in our periphery stepped forward all goo-goo-eyed. "Hi, Ian," she said softly. She was very feminine in a princessy way—wavy, long, auburn hair, big green eyes, perfect figure. The whole girly, curvy enchilada.

"Hi, Miranda. You feeling better?" To me, he explained, "We came in on the same flight from Dallas." And he undulated his hand to indicate crazy turbulence.

"Thanks for not telling everyone about . . ." She reddened, unable to finish whatever it was she wanted kept secret. That she got sick? Was doing two-to-ten in Texas? That they'd made out?

Ian mimed a zipper across his lip. "What happens at thirty-five thousand feet stays at thirty-five thousand feet."

"Thanks," she said. "You want to eat with us?"

He hesitated, possibly out of courtesy to me, so I said, "My cousin Jess is waiting. Gotta go," and started to leave.

Ian reached for my hand, giving it a firm, warm shake with dazzling eye contact. "Sorry if it seemed like I was getting on your case, Zoe. I don't care if you're a vegan, but may I say, on behalf of the Texas Beef Council, that you should never trust a dude who doesn't eat steak."

With a slight lift of his chin, he indicated Dash.

Two

The rosiness had returned to Jess's cheeks, and her mood seemed much improved when I found her sitting cross-legged on the grass laughing with a curly-headed kid in a Life Is Good T-shirt and a hipster black guy with perfectly coiffed dreads; a white short-sleeve, oxford-cloth shirt buttoned right up to the throat; skinny jeans; and ironic, if expensive, Ray-Ban Wayfarer sunglasses, color red.

"How'd it go?" she asked as I came over with my fruit and coffee. I was dying to replay my conversation with Ian, including his zinger of a parting line, but this was not the place, unfortunately, so all I could do was raise my brows—our signal to talk later.

"Zoe, this is Karl," she said, gesturing to the curly-headed kid. "He's from Maine, and he's exhausted because he had to get up at two a.m. to catch a flight here from Boston."

Karl was laid flat on the ground, eyes closed to the sun. "I'd get up to introduce myself, but I'd probably just pass out."

His voice was a strangely high falsetto.

"Don't bother," I said, plunking myself next to him. "Been there."

"And this here is RJ." Jess patted the arm of the hipster. "It's his second summer at Fairyland, since he was an intern the year before. Now he's an RA in the boys' dorm and going to Columbia in the fall."

"Don't forget the Fairyland Executive Training Program," Karl murmured.

Jess said, "Oh, yeah. RJ's in the Fairyland Executive Training Program because he was such an awesome intern the year before."

RJ leaned over and extended his hand. "Ask me anything. I'm here to help."

It was all I could do not to loosen that top button. How could he wear a collar that tight?

"He's Mr. Fairyland," mumbled Karl, who seemed to be half asleep. "He picked me up at the airport, and by the end of the drive I knew to avoid the Chef's Surprise and where to chill in the park after-hours and that unless I was looking for a killer case of Lyme disease I shouldn't go beyond the Haunted Forest. Oh, and that he'd better not catch me with a girl in my room after ten."

With a nod RJ said, "Yes, I'm the one you're gonna want to avoid when you're sneaking out at four in the morning."

A quick wit, I thought approvingly as I sipped my coffee.

"Seriously," Jess said. "That's one of the rules. No girls in the boys' dorms past ten and vice versa."

Karl yawned. "Quit talking about dorms. I couldn't sleep one wink on my flight. All I want to do is take a nap. When are they going to give us our cast assignments?"

"I can tell you now, if you want," RJ said, pulling out a slip of paper from his back pocket. "Obermann, Karl. You're a Red Riding Hood wolf."

Karl let out a moan. "A wolf costume. That'll be so hot. And not in a good way."

"Yeah, but it's also cool," RJ said. "Don't you know? Kids go crazy for a predator in heels and a nightgown."

Jess tried to read over his shoulder. "Do you have everyone's assignments there?"

"Most of them." He ran his finger down the list. "Except yours, Zoe. Next to your name, it says Character Yet to Be Determined."

I knew it—a mistake!

"Ooooh. That's my favorite," Jess teased. "Goldilocks and the Three Characters Yet to Be Determined."

I said, "Shut up! You're just jealous because you wanted to be a Character Yet to Be Determined, too."

Jess cocked her head. "In a way, at our age, Zoe, we're *all* characters waiting to be determined."

"Don't get philosophical on me, Swynkowski." I bit into a slice of cantaloupe and turned to RJ. "What does it mean that I don't have a part? Is that bad?"

"It means they hadn't cast you by the time they were drawing up this list."

Jess went, "Duh."

"Now, let's see. Swynkowski." RJ squinted at the bottom of the paper. "Ah. Here it is."

Jess slapped her hands over her ears. "Don't tell me."

"Red Riding Hood Number Two."

Not even a #1. Bummer.

Jess slumped. "I told you it was bad when they didn't put me in the Princess Tower."

"Buck up. At least you're not a generic elf," I said, rubbing her back. "Anyway, who knows? You might end up loving it."

RJ folded up his paper. "That's a great character. What's your problem?"

I knew Jess didn't feel like going into it, so I said,

"My cousin really wanted to be a princess . . . for a better chance to win the Dream and Do grant."

The Dream & Do grant was the big perk of being a Fairyland summer intern. While high school summer cast members weren't compensated with more than free room and board, at the end of the internship, two of us—a boy and a girl—who'd showed "exceptional Wow!™ spirit" would each receive twenty-five thousand dollars in cash, along with a chance to enter the Fairyland Executive Training Program at Fairyland's parent corporation—Die Über Wunderbar—in Düsseldorf, Germany.

Jess and I didn't talk much about the Dream & Do grant since, obviously, we couldn't *both* win the big cash prize. Of course, being ever sweet, Jess insisted she wanted me to win, so I could pay off Mom's lingering medical bills, but I knew she was counting on the money for college, and I couldn't blame her.

NYU's Tisch School of the Arts, the first step in Jess's dream to become an actor, didn't come cheap, and financial aid was slim. Since the Swynkowskis were currently broke, Tisch would be totally out of the question without some cash to offset the student loans.

In my opinion, this was a no-brainer—Jess *had* to win this grant—though, she was right, being cast as Red Riding Hood didn't help.

RJ nudged her with his elbow. "It doesn't matter what

role you get. It matters how you play it and if you show that Wow! spirit."

Jess sighed. "I highly doubt that. Everyone knows the grants always go to the princes and princesses."

"Maybe you'll be the first to break the mold," he said. "I was a summer intern last year, so I know what Management's looking for: cast members who put their all into playing their parts because, to them, Fairyland is more than a place to work, it's a family."

Jess plucked a few blades of grass, thinking. "Well, I guess it's not the worst part in the world to get. I could be a . . ."

"*Watch* it," warned Karl, whom we'd assumed was asleep.

". . . little pig," Jess added. "Certainly I'd be thrilled to be a wolf. And Zoe, you always said I looked fabulous in red." She batted her lashes.

"Better you than your bank balance." Which I hoped wasn't hitting too close to home, since Jess's checking account had been overdrawn a lot lately.

Manic clapping on the part of Andy the Summer Cast Coordinator forced us to quit talking and pay attention. "We have a lot to do today, cast members, so let's get started," he announced. "Listen up, because this is important!"

After breakfast we were to divide into our character groups and then we were going to take a quick tour through the underground tunnels—or "funnels," as he called them—that led from secret doors in various exhibits around the park down to Our World, where cast members hung out, ate, dressed, etcetera. After that we'd unpack, get settled, and start our official training.

"And now, some ground rules." Andy put up a poster:

THE FAIRYLAND KINGDOM FIVE COMMANDMENTS

1) *There is no such answer as "I don't know" in the Fairyland Kingdom. If a guest asks you a question and you don't know the answer—find it. Conversely, if a guest asks you, "When is the five o'clock parade?" respond politely.*

2) *Make a "no" moment into a "Wow!™" moment. Your job is to spread joy and glee for all to see! So if you spot a guest who's not having fun, turn that frown upside down!*

3) *Pointing is ALWAYS done with two fingers and an open palm. Remember: Give a thumbs-up for Fairyland!*

4) *If a guest gives you trouble, fold your arms genie-style and security will come to your aid. Do not argue, threaten, challenge, or intimidate guests. Guests are RIGHT until proven otherwise. Remember: In Fairyland Kingdom THE GLASS SLIPPER ALWAYS FITS!*

5) *Finally, and most important, TO FAIRYLAND
   ALWAYS BE TRUE. Fairyland is your family
   away from home, so pitch in and help out. We're all
   in this together!*

Then he explained why princes and princesses needed
to learn to look, act, talk, and—when it came to autographs—even write alike so kids wouldn't figure out that,
for example, the Cinderella greeting them in the park in
the morning was different from the one waving good-bye
at night.

"Think back to that awful day when you first realized
the Santa Claus at the mall wasn't the same as the Santa
Claus on TV." Andy shook his head as if this were a tragedy of epic proportions. "We don't want that to happen
with our young guests. *Ever.* We want them to leave convinced that all their favorite fairy-tale characters really do
live happily ever after in Fairyland. And that this is the
only place they call home."

A dig, I assumed, at the Mouse who ruled over the
"other theme park."

The rest of the rules could be found in the handbook.
There were 270, according to Andy, and it was in our best
interest to memorize them all.

With orientation over, it was the moment we'd all been
waiting for: casting. Andy read through the list starting

with the least desirable characters: the animals—aka furries, like Karl—and working his way up the Fairyland pecking order. Jess and a girl named Alice were the two Red Riding Hoods. Ian was the only Puss 'n Boots, which was a surprise, since I'd pegged him for a prince.

When they got to royalty, I started to panic, since I knew I couldn't be one of the "Fab Four"—Cinderella, Snow White, Rapunzel, or Sleeping Beauty—and that my friendship with Jess would be forever ruined if I were. And yet what else could I be?

I watched Dash take his place as a Prince Charming for Sleeping Beauty, and finally the Cinderellas were named—Simone and Adele, two blondes who, in my opinion, were not nearly as pretty as Jess.

And that was it. Apparently my character was still being determined.

"Okay, people, grab your packets," Andy was saying.

I raised my hand. "Um. You didn't call me."

"Zoe Kiefer, right?" Andy brought out an iPad and began typing rapidly. "Oh my. It says here you've been designated as the lady-in-waiting."

Was that even a legit character? I turned to Jess, who had no clue. "What's a lady-in-waiting do?"

"Only everything." Andy pulled out a radio and said something about me going to see the Queen. "Didn't you receive the memo in your email?"

"What memo?" I hadn't been sent anything besides a stack of waivers promising not to drink or take drugs or "publicly disclose, disseminate, or disperse" details about the internship, whatever the heck that meant.

Beads of perspiration sprang from Andy's forehead. "Okay, okay. We can deal." He put his hands on my shoulders and physically rotated me toward the Princess Palace. "Just go see her now in her office. She's waiting." He rattled off reminders as he escorted me down the sparkling fairy path. "It's best not to sit unless she tells you to. Or speak until spoken to. And when she does speak, address her as ma'am."

"Ma'am," I repeated, totally baffled by this entity called the Queen. Surely he couldn't have meant Snow White's evil stepmother, who dressed in purple robes and whom everyone booed in the daily parade.

"Her dog is Tinker Bell." He closed his eyes prayerfully. "Tinker Bell is her pride and joy. We all love Tinker Bell."

I made a mental note.

"You might think your job in the parade is to toss candy, but really it's to guard Her Majesty from tossed apples that are thrown by"—he made a face—"*ingrates* who don't know any better. Remember, don't duck, *catch.*"

"Don't duck, *catch.* Got it."

"And whatever you do, don't mention *the Mouse*."

We got to the drawbridge over the moat that ringed the gigantic, glittering, purple palace with its colorful flags against the brilliant blue sky. Andy pointed (two fingers, one thumb up) to the far turret, where supposedly the Queen sat in her office. My heart fluttered at the prospect of what lay ahead.

"Just tell the trolls I sent you, and you'll be fine."

Trolls. *There were trolls?*

"Good luck," Andy said, with an encouraging pat. "The Queen chose you herself, which means she must have been struck by something in your application. All you have to do is what she says, on time and cheerfully, and never, ever, *ever* break the most important rule—to Fairyland always be true!"

"What does that even mean?" I asked, but it was too late. Andy had hurried off, and I was on my own.

Three

Trolls turned out to be shorthand for *patrols*, Fairyland's in-house rent-a-cops, who perused the park in dark-green jumpsuits and snappy caps on the lookout for lost kids, dropped gum wrappers, and, I suppose, the occasional Mouse Mole (spies who worked for the Mouse). Not for nothing was Fairyland rated #1 in Safe Theme Parks, though after the hassle the trolls gave me at the elevator to the Queen's office, it seemed they might have had a *leeeetle* too much power in their white-gloved hands.

I took the elevator to the fourth floor. It opened to a stark white hallway at the end of which was a frosted-glass door marked simply:

FAIRYLAND KINGDOM Inc.
PINELAND, NEW JERSEY

Behind the door was your average, everyday office painted a calming sage green and with three chairs, a coffee table littered with magazines, a potted fern, and a blue watercooler.

The only difference from my dad's boring accounting office was that here the walls were lined with framed photos of park highlights—the princes and princesses dancing on the stage outside the Princess Palace; Humpty Dumpty sitting on his wall talking to a group of children; Hansel and Gretel pushing a witch into the oven; all seven of the dwarfs hugging Snow White at her cottage; and, front and center, Cinderella and her Prince Charming, cheek to cheek.

A huge plaque that read Fairyland Kingdom . . . Wow!™ in glittering gold letters hung over the large desk where a woman with short brown hair and a flowered shirt sat picking at a blueberry muffin on a napkin. She was the spitting image of Mrs. Herman, our high school's attendance person.

"Excuse me. I'm Zoe Kiefer," I said, unsure as to whether this was the dreaded Queen. "Andy told me I should see you."

The woman brushed crumbs from her desk. "I didn't

ask to see you. You probably mean . . . *her*. Let me buzz."

"So you're not—"

"Lord, no. I'm just Evelyn, her secretary." She emitted a light titter and said into the phone, "Ma'am, I have someone here to see you. A Zoe . . . Yes. I'll send her right in."

There was a *buzzzz*, and a part of the wall slid open. The door had been completely hidden, like something out of a spy movie.

"Good luck!" Evelyn said.

I wish people would stop saying that, I thought as the hidden door closed behind me and I stepped into mission control. That was what popped into my brain when I saw the wall of monitors displaying every aspect of the park in black-and-white. Five rows of ten. Fifty in all. And in front of them sat the strangest figure in a high-backed, black chair poring over a stack of papers at her glass desk.

She said nothing, and I remained standing with my hands behind my back, since Andy had said I shouldn't sit until she gave me permission, though that didn't seem to be coming any time soon. In fact, it was difficult to discern if this creature knew I was there, so engrossed was she in sorting through the piles of paperwork, her spidery fingers slipping in and out of the pages as if she were spinning a web.

Her gown was a luminescent shade of deep violet. A

gold crown was perched on a tasseled red pillow nearby. Her hair, sleek and black like a cat's, had been cut in a downward bob probably to minimize her freakishly long white neck on top of her stick-thin body. The room smelled oddly of overheated electronics, tea, and rosewater perfume.

I cleared my throat, and she lifted a finger. At last she went, "A-ha!" and removed a manila file marked Kiefer, Zoe. She flipped it open and ran her black lacquered nail over what I recognized with some trepidation as my application. Now and then she'd go, "Hmmm" or make a note with a red pen in the margins. Every two seconds she twirled to check the screens before twirling back to her desk, whereupon she continued to read. It was very unnerving because she was reading about me.

There was a tiny *yip!* from a fluffy white dog no bigger than a hand puppet that was curled on a purple satin pillow with a matching purple bow in her hair. This must have been the famous Tinker Bell.

The Queen snapped the file shut and whipped off her half glasses to reveal a pair of black eyes under similarly black arched eyebrows. Her lips were painted in two tones of crimson and violet. "Zoe Kiefer, let me have a look at you."

I stepped back and she said, "Hmm, hmm. Do you exercise?"

"Not lately. Except for gym class." (And not even then if I can help it.)

"Lately. You mean since your mother died." This was said matter-of-factly, as if we were discussing that it might rain.

"Yes . . . ma'am."

"Pity, that." She bit the end of her glasses, scrutinizing. "It says in your application that when you were small, your mother took you to Storytown, and that it was your most favorite place on earth. Is that true?"

Before there was Fairyland Kingdom, there was Storytown, a rinky-dink nursery-rhyme theme park with a petting zoo and swan boats for the juice-box-and-animal-cracker set. We'd go on Wednesday afternoons when New Jersey residents could get in free, and Mom would read me fairy tales by a willow overlooking the moat around Cinderella's Castle. I'd written my application essay on those trips and how I remembered them as the happiest moments with my mother before she got ill. It was sappy, but there you have it. Storytown would always hold a treasured place in my heart, even though it had been bulldozed over long ago.

I nodded. "Yes. I loved that place. I'm sorry that it's gone."

She pointed at the gold necklace at my throat with its single pearl. "Is that your mother's?"

Absently I reached for the chain. "Yes. My father gave it to her the day I was born."

"Hmm, hmm." She nodded and stood. I was surprised to see she had me by a good two inches. "Zoe Kiefer, I approve. You will be my lady-in-waiting or, in the bland vernacular of the hoi polloi, my personal assistant. Each morning you shall fetch me my breakfast and newspapers, filter my mail, retrieve the complaints, and do whatever bidding I decree."

I swallowed hard, since this was not exactly how I'd envisioned spending my summer, in a darkened control room acting like Igor serving some evil master. Also, the dog. Nevertheless, I said, "Yes, ma'am."

"It is a great honor and privilege to be my assistant, Zoe." She winked at her reflection in an ornate mirror that hung on the opposite wall. "As such, you will be present among my closest circle of advisers and therefore part of an elite club that is privy to restricted information. I will need assurances that you can maintain my strictest confidence."

I couldn't keep a secret to save my life. "Yes, ma'am."

"Of course you will be required to read, understand, and commit to memory all two hundred and seventy Fairyland rules."

"Yes, ma'am."

"Finally, you will accompany me daily in the four

o'clock parade dispensing sugar-based snack products to the clamoring juveniles while deflecting any perishable produce that may or may not be thrown in my direction."

Catch, don't duck. "I understand."

"I will need you to proceed posthaste to Wardrobe so you may be fitted with the appropriate gown. As perhaps you have learned during orientation, Rule Number Six states that no cast members may be present in the park during hours of operation sans costume, and with all your upcoming running hither and thither, you will be no exception. Are we clear?"

I nodded.

"You may go. I expect to see you at eight a.m. tomorrow with my breakfast and newspapers. In the meantime do devote yourself to memorizing the rules."

She returned to her monitors and said nothing else. It was unclear if I was truly free to go.

"Wait. I nearly forgot!" She opened a drawer and rummaged around until she found an iPhone. Clicking it on to make sure it was charged, she nodded in satisfaction and handed it to me along with a heavy brass key.

"This is a master," she said, referring to the key. "It opens any door in the park. Use it with discretion. And this is your telephonic device."

"But I thought we weren't allowed to have anything electronic." That was one of the more disturbing revelations of the internship—no Wi-Fi, no phones, no laptops. In other words, nothing that could be used to communicate with the outside world aside from pen and paper.

"Tut, tut! No arguing." She tick-tocked her index finger. "I do not suffer truculence lightly."

"But I wasn't—"

"This handheld telephonic device is so I may contact you at any hour wherever and whenever I am in need. This summer you will not be your own person, Zoe Kiefer. You will be mine, and the sooner you come to terms with that, the better."

The door slid open, and I was officially dismissed. When I looked back, I could have sworn she was kissing Tinker Bell. On the lips.

Four

Shortly after Jess and I had received our "Wow!™ You're a Summer Cast Member!" acceptances, my grief counselor, Ari, asked if I'd have been as excited about working at a fairy-tale theme park if Mom were healthy and alive. Talk about raining on the proverbial parade.

But that's Ari's job, to urge me to "be mindful" of my actions so I'm "acting in the best interests of Zoe" instead of simply "acting out." At least, that's the party line. Anyway, after I'd quit silently cursing him for being a stinker, I'd tried to think if I would have applied to Fairyland if I'd had a normal upbringing. Really, though, that's like asking a cat if she would have preferred to have been born a dog. I only knew one reality—mine.

Well, mine and Karolynne's from *Teenage Pregnant Nightmare*, but I guess that doesn't count.

Mom got sick when I was eight and died when I was fifteen, so most of my growing up involved emergency trips to the hospital and chemo weeks where all our plans were put on hold while Dad and I tiptoed around the house to keep quiet. Neighbors had to shuttle me back and forth to field-hockey practice. Sleepovers were rare, if ever, except at Jess's.

Meanwhile, Mom got weaker and weaker, and it got harder and harder to remember when she'd been the most popular English teacher at our high school, bopping around her classroom in heavy Doc Martens and flowing skirts, her blond hair flying as she passionately discussed *To Kill a Mockingbird* and quoted Dylan (Bob, not Thomas).

I wished I could have taken one of her classes, because everyone who had her claims she was one of the most fun teachers. There's a plaque now on the blue tiled wall outside her old office dedicated to Mrs. Lisa Kiefer with one line underneath—*It ain't me, babe*. That always tears me up, not just because of the oblique reference to overcoming death, but because I'm reminded that strangers knew her better than I did.

Jess tells me that's not true and prods my memory with stories about strawberry picking and how Mom once literally sewed me into a mermaid costume for Halloween and how we Christmas caroled out of tune. Still, I draw a blank.

That's one of the reasons why I wanted to work at Fairyland for the summer, because Mom used to take me here when I was little and I have this strange feeling that if I stick around, I just might run into her. Not in a ghostly way, more like in a spiritual sense.

Naturally I didn't tell Ari that. I'd just said, "Yes, I'd be excited to work at a fairy-tale theme park, even if Mom were healthy and alive."

And we left it at that.

Jess and I leaned against our door and gave it a shove, practically tumbling over each other when it finally gave way. Our white-painted dorm room was tiny, not much bigger than my walk-in closet at home, and hot and stuffy, with one window that clearly had been locked since last year's interns left in August.

"Oxygen!" Jess panted from her spot on the floor.

Climbing over one of the two beds, I undid the latch and with a Herculean push managed to unstick it. We pressed our faces to the screen, inhaling the sweet, fresh air wafting up from Fiddler's Green below.

"We should have brought a fan," Jess said, taking another breath. "This place is going to be sweltering in July."

I'd see if I could wheedle one out of maintenance. Or

maybe Jess's parents could bring one when they stopped by next week to retrieve the Bobmobile, because she was right. No way would we survive a heat wave in these conditions.

The room was barely big enough for a closet and two single beds with drawers underneath. Amenities were few—an electric alarm clock, an overhead light, a smoke detector, two sets of stiff white sheets, two scratchy green blankets, and two rather lumpy pillows. So much for the glamour of living in a wing of the Princess Palace.

"I'm surprised it's not air-conditioned," I said, claiming the bed against the wall so Jess could have the window. Having suffered from asthma as a kid, Jess needed all the extra ventilation she could get.

Jess got down the sheets and blankets from the top shelf in the closet. "It's only the Ordinary Cast Members dorms that don't have air. Every other building in the park does, including the royal turrets. I was talking to Simone at lunch, and she said her room was huge, with a window seat and even her own TV."

"That hardly seems fair," I said, trying to decide which sheet to use on the bottom, since neither was fitted. Already, I could picture us tossing and turning as the sheets bunched around our ankles while the princes and princesses slept soundly in the cool comfort of sixty-eight degrees.

"They have maid service, too. People who pick up their socks and make their beds. Also, huge bathrooms with cut flowers and free hair spray and great lighting."

Jess kept her head down, neatly tucking in the corners of her blanket just so. She was trying to be a good sport about not being a princess, but I could tell that even after RJ's motivational speech, she was still bummed. Not exactly the joyful kickoff I'd hoped for.

I said, "Don't give up. There's still a chance that you could be promoted. Someone could drop out or bomb or decide being a princess is too much work."

"Not likely." Jess slid on a pillowcase.

I'd essentially given up on the whole settling-in thing and was lying on the one sheet staring up at the cracked ceiling. "You never know."

"Yes, I do. During the tour of Our World this morning, I overheard that the only way to be cast as a prince or a princess is by going to one of those Fairyland summer camps as a kid. The closest one costs more than five thousand dollars per session."

I let out a whistle. "What a rip-off."

"Not if you win the twenty-five-thousand-dollar grant. Then you come out twenty thousand dollars ahead. But you can't win the grant unless you spend five grand on camp so . . ." She threw up her hands.

"The rich get richer."

"Exactly." Jess threw the pillow on her bed. "All I can do is what RJ suggested: pump so much Wow! spirit into playing Red Riding Hood that Management has no choice but to give me that freaking grant." Then, catching herself, she quickly added, "Not that you don't deserve it, too, Zoe."

"It's okay," I said, because it really was. And I resolved that somehow, some way, I would use my new connection to the Queen to make sure Jess got her wish, since there had to be some fringe benefit to waiting on an obviously crazy woman 24-7.

Five

I sprang out of bed the next morning with renewed energy to become the most kick-butt lady-in-waiting ever. One month of my impeccable service and the Queen would be so awed by my efficiency that she'd insist on repaying her gratitude. And what better way than by placing a crown on my cousin's delicate head?

I said nothing to Jess, who was fast asleep when I tiptoed out of bed at dawn to shower and be in Wardrobe by six thirty, a full hour and a half before I had to bring the Queen her breakfast. The early bird gets the worm!

I took the elevator down to Our World, the underground complex maze of polished white hallways that led to the cafeteria; the rec room with games, card tables, a few couches, a soda machine, and one big flat-screen TV;

the gym, where princes and princesses were working out even this early; Personnel; and, finally, Wardrobe.

Trish—the frazzled, red-haired stylist who'd taken my measurements the day before—looked up from her morning Sudoku in shock.

"You're surprised, right?" I handed her a cheese Danish that I'd thoughtfully procured from the cafeteria, seeing as how she wouldn't get a break this morning, what with all the new interns coming and going with various costume malfunctions. "I'm an hour early." I grinned, awaiting her approval.

Trish checked the clock on the wall. "Actually you're late."

"Late?" My grin instantly deflated. "But the Queen doesn't need to see me until eight."

"Oh, that's what she says. That's not what she means." Trish put aside the Danish and headed to the racks and racks of costumes in the back. "You'll have to learn that what the Queen says and what she means bear absolutely no resemblance."

A dull headache, the very beginning of one, seeped into my temples as I watched Trish flick her pink nails over the hangers. I'd had my fingers crossed for something pretty, a silky emerald-green gown to go with my eyes, perhaps. Instead, Trish held out a demure dove gray.

"Cannot upstage Her Majesty," she said, removing the hanger.

Minutes later I was dressed and seated while Helga applied thick makeup that felt and smelled like orange mud. My skin flamed in protest. Years of Neutrogena and faithful use of non-oil-based foundation and now this. An assault!

When she was done, I looked in the mirror and barely recognized my pale face with its huge eyes and glossy lips under severely parted hair that had been pulled so tightly, the tiny blue veins on my forehead throbbed. The pearl tiara perched on top of my updo only added to the insanity.

"A true lady-in-waiting," Helga decided, capping her mascara with satisfaction. "You could have served in Henry the Eighth's court."

I checked my neck for reassurance that it was still in one piece and, gathering my dress, thanked the crew and hightailed it to the cafeteria, where I found Dash, he of the hemp bracelets, completely unfamiliar in his Sleeping Beauty Prince Charming costume of a navy jacket, white sash, and silver crown.

His already ruddy cheeks reddened even more. "Don't even say it."

"No, you're fine!" I exclaimed, trying to keep a straight face though it had just hit me that he was the spitting image of a Prince Charming Ken doll Jess got for her sixth birthday. "You look extremely . . ."

"Lame."

It didn't help that his wavy hair had been slicked into some old-fashioned pompadour.

"Let's put it this way: The ten-and-under set will find you adorable."

He winced, and I realized it was a stupid thing to say, because what seventeen-year-old guy wants to be adored by little kids?

"Just to set the record straight, you should know that I once hiked one hundred and sixty miles of the Pacific Crest Trail by myself," he said, "in seven days."

"I'm sure. And you drive a monster truck and chop your own wood."

"And change my own oil."

I started to laugh, when I detected a strange, not unpleasant, in fact quite pleasant, aroma—a cross between my dad's spicy aftershave and the overpowering flowers that had filled our house after Mom died.

Seeing me wrinkle my nose, Dash said, "It's the Prince Charming cologne."

"The what?"

"Apparently it's made from rare Amazonian orchids. They keep it under lock and key in Wardrobe just for the princes, because it has, um, certain powerful phero-mones."

In other words chemicals secreted outside the body in order to elicit a response—fear, lust, hunger, distaste—in others. That had been on the AP bio test I'd just taken.

"You're kidding right?" I checked myself to see if the Prince Charming cologne was affecting my behavior. Nope. Not yet, anyway.

"It's pathetic." He shook his head and grabbed a blue plastic tray, handing it to me before taking one for himself. "Andy said the cologne's a must-have for working the Princesses Royal Table at the resort, even at breakfast."

That's where Dash was headed, to the official Fairyland Kingdom Resort, where for thirty dollars per person (twenty dollars for kids), you could eat pancakes and eggs while dancing with the Fab Four princesses and their significant princely others. Seemed like a mighty high price to pay for what was essentially the $6.99 Rooty Tooty Fresh 'N Fruity down at IHOP, but that was the Fairyland Kingdom Resort for you—*cha-ching*!

At the coffee bar, I put in a request for a Fairyland Caramel Coconut Latte—Fairyland's signature drink—that I was sure the Queen would appreciate. "I've heard those breakfasts are reserved for weeks. Should be a blast."

Dash grabbed a paper cup and flipped the lever for regular. "I don't know if it's a blast, but it's necessary if you want to win the Dream and Do grant. RJ said the princes who bag the breakfasts essentially disqualify themselves."

I selected a luscious chocolate croissant for the Queen along with a raspberry yogurt with fresh raspberries. The Queen's breakfast was going to be spectacular.

"The yogurt's not almond, you know," he said, taking a sip. "And technically, the chocolate and butter in the croissant aren't vegan, either."

"They're not for me. They're for my boss, the Queen. I'm her personal assistant." The coffee barista handed me the latte with a heart-shaped swirl of froth while Dash studied me with new interest.

"I swear," I said, capping the latte. "Not for me. I know it has real cream in it."

He waved his hand, like the vegan angle had no relevance. "I was thinking about your cast assignment. It's not really a role, is it? You just work for her."

"Aside from appearing in the parade by her side to throw candy." And catch the rotten apples, though I judiciously kept this to myself.

"But nothing else. You're not a witch or a Gretel or anything?"

"That's right." I swiped my ID, which was how we cast members paid for food. "Why?"

"I dunno. It's interesting." He swiped his ID, too. "Does that mean you have a better chance of winning the grant because you'll be working so closely with her? Or a worse chance?"

This was his second reference to the twenty-five-thousand-dollar grant in almost as many minutes, a fact that I supposed was significant. "I have no idea. I haven't thought about it since I'm not a prince or a princess, and everyone knows you've got to be royalty to win. So you're lucky."

He walked me down the hall to the elevator. "Not that lucky. Altogether, there are sixteen princes and princesses. We've all had the same training and have the same credentials, and our parents, who've shelled out thousands of bucks to send us to the right camps, expect us to come home with the grant, so there's the guilt factor if we don't." He punched the button to the elevator that would take me to the Queen's office and him to the ground floor of the Princess Palace. "My dad's last words when he dropped me off at the airport were, 'Think about it, Dash, we could have taken the whole family to Europe for what we've spent on you.'"

Ouch! I hadn't considered the parent angle. My own father wouldn't have known what a Fairyland camp was if you'd driven him there and dumped him off smack under Jack's Beanstalk. "It can't be that bad."

"You don't know. Up in the royal turrets, the cutthroat instinct's so strong, you can almost taste it. No one trusts anyone." The elevator opened, and we got in. "Just be glad you're not one of us, Zoe, because at least you'll get to enjoy your summer. Me? I'll be fighting to make sure I don't go home a loser."

Six

I was so early for work that Evelyn wasn't in yet, her pink cotton cardigan neatly draped over the back of her chair, which had been pushed under her desk, her computer off. Even the morning's newspapers were still stacked in their blue plastic baggies.

I'll take these, I thought, unwrapping the newspapers and laying them flat next to several oversize pink peonies I'd plucked from behind the Princess Palace for a whoosh of June flora.

Best. Assistant. Ever.

Brimming with pride, I knocked on the wall, where I guessed the door was hidden. "It's me, your . . . ma'am," I said, catching myself. The door slid open, and I presented the tray. "Breakfast!"

The Queen spun around from her monitors. "Zoe! How nice of you to put in an appearance."

She peered at the tray as if it contained lab specimens. "And what would you like me to do with . . . this?" she asked, fluttering her hand over the croissant. "*Eat* it or just attach it to my thighs?"

My bubble of confidence went *pop!* as it occurred to me that I'd somehow made a mistake. "It's just a pastry."

"It's packed with calories. As is that." She flared her nostrils at the Caramel Coconut Latte. "A week's worth. Not to mention it would send me into diabetic shock. Are you trying to kill me, Zoe?"

A bead of sweat ran down the back of my neck. "No, ma'am."

"Where did you get those flowers?"

"From outside the . . ."

She brought a skeletal hand to her chest in distress. "Don't tell me you took them from *our* gardens."

"The one behind the palace." I was now so nervous, my palms were leaving wet sweat marks on the tray. "There are tons of flowers there—*hundreds*—I figured no one would ever notice three missing blooms by the exhaust vents."

"No one would notice! Did you not read your rules as I instructed, Zoe? Number One-Eighty-Three: *No flora or fauna on the property of Fairyland Kingdom Inc.*

shall be cut, trampled, or mutilated in any manner without written approval of Fairyland Kingdom Management upon penalty of a five-hundred-dollar fine."

Crap! I didn't have money to pay a five-hundred-dollar fine.

She turned to her computer, called up a file, and clicked her nails across the keyboard. "Instead of a pecuniary penalty, I will be lenient and mark one demerit. Two demerits, and you will be removed as my assistant. Three, and you will be sent home posthaste without a college recommendation and/or reference of any positive nature. Are we clear?"

For *picking flowers*? It was so randomly unfair, I felt like bursting into tears. Instead, between gritted teeth, I said, "Yes, ma'am."

"May I ask what on earth were you thinking?"

My arms were beginning to ache. Those newspapers were not light. "I was thinking that I'd spruce up your morning. I was trying to make you happy. You know, fresh-cut flowers . . . *Wow!*"

She let out a long, pained sigh. "What would make me happy is a pot of Earl Grey tea. . . . For heaven's sake, Zoe, put down that tray and take some notes."

With no obvious place to put it, I set the tray on the floor and scrambled for a notepad. (Should have thought to bring one. Stupid!)

Exasperated, the Queen ended up finding one in a drawer and handing me a pen. "For future reference, the office supplies are behind you in the closet."

I turned. The wall was flat and bare. There was no closet, just like there was no door.

". . . Three almonds, whole, unsalted and raw; one hard-boiled egg, no yolk."

She was dictating. I flipped open the pad, scratched the pen to get the ink going, and jotted down what she'd said so far: *Earl Grey. Almonds. One hard-boiled egg, no yolk* . . . I looked up. "How is that possible, without a yolk?"

"Is this a cooking class?" Her black eyes glittered.

"No, ma'am."

"Ask Chef. He knows. Other than that, I will say the fresh raspberries you brought are acceptable." She bent down to reach for the berries and gasped. *"Tinkers!"*

Tinker Bell had silently slipped off her satin pillow and was going to town on the chocolate croissant.

"Well," I said, smiling, "at least someone appreciates it."

The Queen seized her precious baby in horror, frantically wiping her dog's mouth with a lace doily. "Chocolate will kill her. Don't you know that? It's the theobromine. Positively lethal for canines!"

"Really? Because once our Lab, Molly, got to my

Christmas stocking before I did and ate all my chocolate Santas, and nothing happened." I glared at Tinker Bell. Yes, she was just a dog, but I couldn't help feeling she was trying to get me in trouble. "I'm sure Tinker Bell will be fine."

"Only if you take her to the Fairyland vet, Dr. Venderbraugh, immediately. His office is by the stables." The Queen thrust Tinker Bell into my arms. "Tell him you tried to poison her."

"I didn't try to—"

"Ah, ah, ah." There was that tick-tocking finger again. "No truculence." The door slid open. "Posthaste!"

Clearly I had no choice but to go. In the outer office, I nearly ran smack into Evelyn, who had just arrived, blueberry muffin in hand. She took one look at the dog trying to lap up every last bit of deliciousness with her tiny pink tongue and said, "I don't wanna know. By the way, did you take my newspapers?"

"Those are yours? I thought they were the Queen's."

"And you just handed them to her willy-nilly?" Evelyn lowered her voice. *Unedited?*"

My mind went blank. I scrambled to remember the rule about newspapers. "I'm sorry. I'll try to fix it. Right now I have to get Tinker Bell to Dr. Venderbraugh."

"Okay. I'll see what I can do. Let's just hope she hasn't opened to the entertainment section and seen the Mouse.

If that happens . . ." She nodded to the invisible door. "Honey, I'm afraid you won't last the day."

The stables were located at the edge of Fairyland near the garage, about as far as you could go in the park before coming to the stone wall marked with signs warning:

NO PEEKY BOOS BEYOND THIS POINT!

Under which was a drawing of Cinderella, winking.

I didn't know what was beyond the perimeter wall that would make someone want to take a "Peeky Boo." As far as I could tell, only more New Jersey scrub pine. However, during our orientation tour, Andy had mentioned that the Haunted Forest—where Hansel and Gretel, Snow White, and the witches hung out—abutted what he called the Forbidden Zone, which we were never to enter.

The Forbidden Zone was swampy like the rest of the Pinelands and riddled with huge spiders and ticks carrying Lyme disease, Andy had said. Also snakes, including poisonous timber rattlers that Fairyland Maintenance worked like "the Dickens" to remove from the park.

"As long as you stay in the Haunted Forest, you're okay," he'd said. "But never, ever go over or under the metal fence and beyond. It's an automatic elimination from the program and, needless to say"—he'd paused to implant us with a meaningful look—"from winning the Dream and Do grant."

Frankly, the dude had me at *snakes* and *huge spiders*. Expulsion from the program was peanuts in comparison.

It was understandable why Fairyland stuck the red wooden stables all the way out there. They stank. This was also where they kept the Three Little Pigs, the Three Billy Goats Gruff, along with a Tortoise and a Hare during the off-season. I'd have given anything for those Princess Palace peonies right about now.

The vet's office was closed, but when I went around to the stables I found a blond prince anxiously perched atop a beautiful old white horse and—by their side in a T-shirt, dirty jeans, and muck boots—Ian.

"Now, Marcus, what you're going to do is just walk her around the stable, okay?" Ian was saying, one hand on the thick brown leather saddle.

Marcus, in the white jacket and red epaulets of a Cinderella Prince Charming, clutched the reins and swallowed. "What if I fall off?"

"You won't fall off. Little kids ride her," Ian said patiently. "At birthday parties. With their grandmothers. That's why you have Lulu, because she's gentle."

For her part, Lulu stood placidly chewing on her bit. She rolled one of her golf-ball eyes at Tinker Bell, and

Tinker Bell twitched in fear before activating a full-body tremor.

"It's okay," I said as Tink kicked her tiny legs, struggling to leap out of my arms and cause more mischief, probably by scurrying around the horse's hooves and causing her to canter. I clutched her tightly and whispered, "Oh, no you don't."

"Zoe?" Ian squinted, like he couldn't make out the real me through the makeup. "What're you doing here?" He ran a hand through his black hair, grinning, obviously pleased to see me.

I flashed an apologetic smile at Marcus, who'd given up the reins and was pitched forward, hugging the saddle. Despite the barnyard stench, his princely cologne of pungent Amazonian orchids wafted toward me and, unlike my first experience with Dash, I almost swooned. Perhaps its effects were cumulative. Or maybe Marcus, knowing he could use all the help he could get, had laid on the pheromones a little too thick.

"Sorry to interrupt," I said, stepping away from the cologne to clear my thoughts, "but I'm trying to find Dr. Venderbraugh, the vet. Tinker Bell ate some chocolate."

"Did you now?" Ian asked Tink, scratching her between the ears. Tink approved with adoring eyes, the traitor. "How much?"

I couldn't tell what role Ian was playing here, assistant vet or what. "Not much. A lick. Maybe two."

"Ah, that's nothing. If you're really worried, you can give her equal parts water and hydrogen peroxide—in her case, I'd say a tablespoon of each—and she'll—"

"Ian!" Marcus shouted in panic. "The horse! It's moving. Now what do I do? *Ian?*"

Lulu had begun her lazy trot up the path. Honestly, I've seen grannies in walkers with tennis balls on the bottom move faster.

"First take the reins, not the saddle," Ian said.

Marcus wiped sweat off his forehead and, after much mumbling, quickly grabbed the reins. "I hate this. I'm a surfer, not a horse rider. I'm going to fall off and be paralyzed and never get on the board again."

"Dude, chill. Now just let her lead the way. She knows the route. And don't forget!" Ian called. "She's a big, dumb beast." To me, he added in an aside, "They should have a lot in common."

We watched Marcus and Lulu mosey up the path at a snail's pace. "How's he going to survive as Prince Charming if he can't ride a horse?" I asked.

Ian shrugged. "I dunno. He's supposed to be galloping through the park to meet Cinderella before the dance. At this rate she'll be lucky if he makes it to her retirement party."

"And even though you're Puss 'n Boots you're helping him because . . ."

"Because Scott the equestrian trainer is working with

the other princes who aren't so afraid. Having grown up on my dad's ranch in Colorado, I'm pretty good with large animals and tourists who've never ridden."

"This would be the ranch with the cannibalistic chickens?"

Ian brightened. "I'm telling you, don't mess. They're vicious. Kind of like our Queen, from what I hear. Is she really as hideous as everyone says?"

"I'll let you decide," I said. "This morning, after I brought her a chocolate croissant, she accused me of attempting to kill her dog."

"And were you?"

"What?"

"Trying to kill her dog?"

I was shocked by the question, though Ian was laughing like the Queen wasn't a threat at all.

"Seriously, you have no idea," I said, launching into how I'd tried to be the perfect assistant, only to be a complete disaster. "I cannot screw up again, or I'll get one more demerit and be out of the program, guaranteed."

"I don't believe it. She's just scaring you since it's the first day."

"She's not. She's out to get me." I held up Tinker Bell. "And her little dog, too. I need advice on what to do."

Ian wiped his hand on a dirty rag, thinking. "How about this? Ask RJ. He knows everything about this park, and maybe he can get in touch with one of the Queen's former assistants who could give you the lowdown. You know, he does have internet access, so it's possible."

That was not a bad idea. Not a bad idea at all. "Thanks, Ian. I—"

There was a loud *thump!* followed by a worrisome *"Oww!"* We froze.

"Ian?" Marcus wailed from the other side of the stable. "Dude, I think I just broke my ass."

Seven

RJ was not entirely enthusiastic about tapping former cast members for advice on how to please the Queen, since, as a resident assistant, he was supposed to be upholding the rules, not breaking them.

"What happens in Fairyland stays in Fairyland," he said. "Rule Number One Hundred Fifty." Then he went on about the "importance of confidentiality" and "above all, to Fairyland be true," blah, blah, blah. That was until I explained that I needed to worm my way into Her Majesty's good graces so I could get Jess promoted to princess and she could win the Dream & Do grant and go to college.

"I'll do what I can, but you should know it doesn't

work that way. Regular cast members are hardly ever crowned," he said as we sat on the lily pad in the Frog Prince's Pond, where I'd asked him to meet me after the park closed. "The princes and princesses were once kids who went to the Fairyland summer camps, where they were intensively trained on how to talk and look and act. That's how it's always been."

"I know that's the party line, but let's give it a shot," I said, playing on my hunch that he was harboring a crush on my cousin. "Jess will be so grateful to you when I let her know that you bent the rules for me. It shows that even though you're quasi Management, you're a good guy."

His lips twitched into a slight smile.

However, any hope I had of RJ being on our side was soon squashed. Later that week—and miraculously still employed—I was playing The Settlers of Catan in the rec room with Karl (a Catan whiz!) and beating the pants off Marcus the equine-phobic, surf-bum Prince Charming when RJ came in carrying a copy of *Fairyland Kingdom Internship Handbook & Rules.*

"Here," he said, tossing it dismissively into my lap. "You should read these and memorize them before you ask me again to do something inappropriate." Then he went over to the vending machine, plunked in some quarters, and walked off with a Diet Coke.

I was pretty pissed. For starters, I detested the word *inappropriate*, and I resented his implication that he'd decided not to help me after all because rules were rules. But handing me a copy of the handbook in front of my friends was just the sour cherry on top. When I got back to my dorm room, I promptly tossed it in the trash.

"What's this?" Jess asked, pulling it out.

"It's nothing," I said, kicking off my flip-flops. "I already have a copy."

"Of these?" She pointed to several white sheets of paper that had fallen out of the book onto the floor.

I picked up the papers and scanned the contents: three pages of detailed notes on the Queen's quirks, habits, likes, dislikes, and what had worked for ladies-in-waiting before. I grinned, positively ecstatic. This was almost better than getting the cheat sheet to Mr. Ellison's precalc midterm. It was the holy grail of Fairyland!

"What is it?" Jess asked.

"Oh, nothing," I said, tucking the notes under my pillow for late-night reading after she was asleep. "But next time you see RJ, make sure to be super nice."

"Why?"

"Because, of all the guys around here, I have a feeling he's the one who's a true prince."

* * *

As the instructions noted, I was to read, memorize, and then completely destroy the contents by throwing the pages into the incinerator down by the warehouses the next morning before walking Tinker Bell.

This was the first piece of advice—to wake Tinker Bell at dawn, take her for a short stroll, and then return her refreshed and watered to her cashmere doggy bed so the Queen could sleep in. The more the Queen slept, the more pleasant she became.

Ditto for sugar, which Her Majesty (loudly and frequently) pretended to eschew. A teaspoon of honey in her pot of Earl Grey worked like magic, especially if I could get a cup into her before eight. My mystery mentor also advised slipping one tiny square of dark, dark chocolate under her regular lunch of three slices of Bibb lettuce and half a cherry tomato. The chocolate would never be acknowledged, but it would never go uneaten, either.

After one of her temper tantrums, compliment her hair/makeup/skin, my mentor advised. *When she objects, hold up the Magic Mirror on the wall. It was a gift from an aging Hollywood actress and makes any woman, no matter what her age, look beautiful and young.*

Other tips included sorting the mail to cull anything even remotely connected to the Mouse, such as postcards for Mouse-related cruises. Also catalogs showing families vacationing in national parks or by the beach should promptly be ditched. The Queen threw a fit when she read about people spending their summer holidays anywhere besides Fairyland.

The same applied to newspapers, which had to be "edited"—as Evelyn had mentioned—following the same criteria. Even advertisements for church bingos or community potluck dinners were best jettisoned unless, of course, they were being held in the park.

Next was the consumer-complaint box—i.e., the Box of Whine. Every morning the trolls gathered the Fairyland Kingdom Surveys left by the exit gates and dumped them in a locked wooden box by Personnel in Our World. It was in my best interest to read those complaints before the Queen and to filter out any survey that even hinted that the guests' experiences had been less than perfect.

Finally, the notes concluded, *never, ever do or say anything that might be perceived as "disloyal" to Fairyland. This is the Queen's Golden Rule: Above all, to Fairyland be true. Sounds simple enough, except you're never quite sure what the Queen considers an act of treason. As long as you act like you're part of the Fairyland family, she will be your greatest advocate.*

Cross her once . . . and you're dead.

I threw the pages of tips into the incinerator like the author wanted and hugged myself as they burst into bright orange flames.

Loyalty. That was the key. *As long as you act like*

you're part of the Fairyland family, she will be your great-est advocate.

My mentor's words of wisdom saved my butt. The Queen was much more pleasant now that she could sleep in and let me walk Tinker Bell, though I will admit, until I got her that cup of honey-laced Earl Grey, she was a bit of a hag.

After that I did my best to do everything my secret mentor advised. I presented the Queen with only posi-tive reviews glowing with praise. I admired her nails and skin, the deft way she swiveled her chair—anything to boost her ego. I doted on Tinker Bell and earned extra brownie points when I started adding smoked fish eggs— i.e., crazily expensive Russian caviar—to her diet as a way of "improving her coat."

I organized Her Majesty's pencils by length, sorted her shoes by color, arranged for fresh flowers to be deliv-ered daily from the gardener, who did have approval to cut whatever he pleased, and repeatedly confirmed that, *yes, yes*, she really was the fairest of them all.

"Your blatant brownnosing disgusts me," she'd reply, though I could tell she ate it up.

During the evening parades, I caught every piece of fruit while tossing candy with such ease that Her Majesty never realized she was under attack. When she stepped onto the balcony to wave good night, I drowned out the crowd's boos by cranking "There She Is, Miss America" over the loudspeakers. The Queen was so touched, I could have sworn I saw a tear in her eye.

And if I wasn't catering to Her Majesty's every whim, then I was running around the park putting out fires set by the cast.

Marcus, especially, continued to be problematic. Not only did he keep slipping off his horse, but being perpetually jet-lagged and on California time, he often slept through his alarm, thereby requiring me to bang on his door, hollering, "Surf's up!" until he dragged himself out of bed.

Aside from Marcus, everything was going so well that, two weeks into the internship, while I was removing those irritating inserts from her copy of *People* magazine (as well as searching for any reference to the Mouse), the Queen spun around from her monitors and remarked, "Zoe, I must admit that you are not the disaster I feared on the first day. Of course you are still slow, untalented, slightly dim-witted, and, above all, a shameless sycophant, but with training and discipline, I see potential."

I smiled to myself but kept my head down. (Another admonition of my mentor: to avoid direct eye contact whenever possible.) "Thank you, ma'am."

"Your efforts deserve meritorious recompense. Maintain your five-star performance, and I might even remove that flower-picking demerit that hangs over your head like a poisonous weed."

Then she went back to ogling her beloved screens while, internally, I was leaping for joy. All I had to do was keep on keeping on and soon the Queen would grant me a wish, which would be for Jess to be made Cinderella, and we'd live happily ever after!

"Seems your attempts to do me in have failed, huh?" I whispered to Tinker Bell, who was snoozing on her purple satin cushion.

She popped open a tiny, evil black eye. *Grrrrr*, she growled, so softly, it sounded more like a snore.

Little did I know that, within hours, this eight-pound fluff ball of evil would set in motion a series of events intended to trigger my demise. To paraphrase William Congreve, "Hell hath no fury like a bichon frise scorned."

Eight

I was fast asleep when the iPhone the Queen gave me blared the strains of "Every Breath You Take," the creepy Police song about stalking that Jess had set as my ringtone for Her Majesty.

"Zoe! Something's wrong with Tinkers." The Queen sounded panicked. "I've been buzzed."

Strange but true: Tinker Bell had been taught to press her paw on a little brass button that activated a buzzer in the Queen's bedroom. Frankly, I'd had my doubts that a dog with a brain the size of an overgrown peanut could be trained to use such a thing, but, apparently, overgrown-peanut dog brains are wildly underestimated.

Lowering her voice, the Queen explained, "I suspect

she is suffering from an upset tummy. We were celebrating the latest quarterly profit statements this evening, and I'm afraid she overdid it with the foie gras and champagne."

Probably really expensive champagne, too. Stifling a yawn, I said, "Yes, ma'am. I'll be right there." And hung up to get dressed.

Jess rolled over. "You're kidding, right?"

"I wish." Pulling on a pair of shorts, my Bridgewater-Raritan High School hoodie, and flip-flops, I took the iPhone so the Queen wouldn't wake Jess with another call but left the flashlight next to my bed, figuring Tink would require no more than a quick do-si-do around her favorite bush.

Had I any inkling that her plan would be to take off for the Haunted Forest as soon as her toes touched the artificially green grass of Fiddler's Green and that she'd pursue an imaginary squirrel all the way to the fence and I'd be forced to follow her into the Forbidden Zone, where I'd be stuck in quicksand, relying on the assistance of some wise-cracking, rule-breaking, night-wandering prince, I might, indeed, have been more prepared.

But I wasn't.

The following morning I awoke with sand under my nails, the prince's shirt swatch in my hand, and the blurry feeling that my duty was to report the prince's illegal activities—that is, if I were as loyal to the Fairyland family as Her Majesty believed me to be.

Except I couldn't be loyal to the Fairyland family, because I'd promised the prince I wouldn't tell, a vow I absolutely couldn't break. It wasn't just that he'd found Tinker Bell and saved my butt, but that he'd found a branch and saved my life.

"So let me get this straight," Jess said as I opened the Queen's morning newspapers and went directly to the entertainment section to start editing. "You were chasing Tinker Bell, and you found an old wall, and when you reached up to see what it was, you stepped into a sinkhole."

"Quicksand, actually." I pondered whether Her Majesty would be irritated by an ad for a movie about Snow White even though it hadn't been produced by a Mouse studio. "And I more than stepped. I went in up to my thighs." I cut it out just in case.

"That's *sooo* scary. I probably would have screamed my head off."

"And let the trolls find me in the Forbidden Zone with Tink lost? No way."

Jess plunked her finger on a coupon for free kiddie bowling, a family-friendly alternative to visiting Fairyland that would send the Queen into fits. "You missed this."

I uncapped my X-acto knife and proceeded to carve

out the offending ad along with several advertisements for skee-ball arcades, movie theaters, and a local internet café. "Good catch."

"No problem. Give me the inserts, and I'll check the rest."

It was the Sunday paper, so there were tons. I dumped them in the lap of her blue gingham Red Riding Hood dress, and she got down to work.

"Here's what I want to know," Jess said. "What was a prince doing after curfew in, of all places, the Forbidden Zone? I keep thinking of those spiders and snakes and centipedes running around and . . ." She lifted her scissors and shivered.

"I have no idea what he was doing there. Trespassing into the FZ is an automatic dismissal from the program. Why take the risk?" Checking again to make sure no one in the rec room was in listening range, I added, "You know, I never would have been there if it hadn't been for that damned dog."

"Hey, home furries. What's up?" Ian sauntered in, half dressed in his Puss 'n Boots costume followed by Karl and RJ. They flopped down on the couches, and Ian and Karl placed their heads on either side of the newspapers to bug Jess, who was totally creeped out by the way decapitated animal parts lay around Wardrobe like a horror movie.

"See?" Ian said. "They're reading. Just like you."

Jess pushed them to the floor in disgust. "I'm sorry to say that yours still smells like barf, Karl."

"Not my fault. I had no choice."

This was true. One of the little secrets at Fairyland was that because costumes like the wolf's were so mega hot, it was not unheard of for the cast members wearing them to suffer mild heatstroke on sweltering summer days.

This presented a variety of challenges starting with Fairyland Rule #13: *No furry cast member may remove any part of his or her costume in the park during operating hours. Should an emergency arise, the aforementioned character will calmly and quietly exit so as not to draw attention. ONLY then may the costume be removed.*

A few days ago, with temperatures inching into the nineties, Karl got sick while in the Fourth of July parade. With no discreet way to slip into Our World while hundreds of people were taking his photo and asking for hugs, he had to endure the awfulness until the very end, when he was finally allowed to go underground and come out for air. Even though Wardrobe had done what they could with heavy doses of Febreze, it only made the situation worse by covering one bad smell with another. No matter how long he showered after work, he still reeked faintly of Sweet Citrus & Zest and puke.

RJ popped off the lid of his iced tea. "What are you

doing here, Zoe? Usually you're at Her Majesty's beck and call by now."

"The Queen let me sleep in because—" I'd planned on inventing some bogus excuse, but Jess beat me to the punch.

"Because the Queen called her in the middle of the night to go walk Tinker Bell, and, guess what, the dog got past the fence and into the Forbidden Zone, where Zoe fell into quicksand and—"

I gave her a hard pinch under the table before she got to the part about the prince. She promptly clamped her mouth shut.

RJ arched his eyebrow. "*Tsk, tsk*, Zoe. The Forbidden Zone? That's an instant disqualification from winning the Dream and Do grant, you know." He took a sip of his iced tea. "Of course, if you'd memorized the rules like I'd told you . . ."

I gave him a look. "I did. All two hundred and seventy." I gathered up the scraps of newspaper and pushed them into the trash can. "I can't help it if Tinker Bell took off."

Ian got up and quietly closed the doors. "Even if it wasn't your fault, Zoe, you probably shouldn't be blabbing that story all over the place, especially in the presence of a future Fairyland executive over here." He nodded toward RJ.

"Get real, Ian. You know RJ would never fink on us," Jess said, doing that thing where she opens her baby blues and turns guys into mush. "He's stand-up. Aren't you, RJ?"

You could practically see RJ melt like butter. "Yeah, chill, Ian. I'm not *that* much of a creep."

RJ and Jess locked gazes just a trite too long.

Behind their backs, Ian and I rolled our eyes.

Karl, who'd been strangely silent during this exchange, suddenly roused himself from his reverie. "If you ask me, there's something weird about the way Management wants to keep us out of the Forbidden Zone. The Pinelands aren't that dangerous, not like the Everglades in Florida. So what's the big deal?"

Well, I thought, how about quicksand, for starters?

Nine

I arrived at work to find my esteemed commander standing at her desk with a cell phone pressed to her ear, her dark eyes flashing with anger.

As usual she wore her sleek purple gown with its flipped gold collar, her shiny jet-black hair impeccably styled in its severe downward bob, her eyebrows tweezed into constant shock.

". . . Please don't patronize me," her two-toned red-and-violet lips snapped as she impatiently waved for me to deposit her breakfast tray and vanish from sight. "That's not an excuse. That's a flimsy taradiddle, and you know it!"

I put down the tray, but I didn't leave. Instead I poured

her tea and cut her grapefruit sections into the way she preferred, thirty miniscule morsels she could consume while talking. That I dipped each one into a clear pool of sweet agave syrup was a secret I alone knew.

Her Majesty switched ears, and I handed her a tiny grapefruit sliver on a cocktail fork. She took it without thinking. "All right. I'll tolerate your pathetic explanation, but it had better be satisfactory."

I fed her an almond on a silver spoon. She crunched and listened as I carefully patted the corner of her mouth with an authentic French doily. "Yes, well, that's all very logical. Still, it doesn't explain how he got away." I fed her another nut, and she didn't object.

"Tea?" I whispered.

She nodded, and I handed her a cup with a healthy dose of honey. Sipping and sighing, placated by subversive shots of sucrose, she finally collapsed into her high-backed chair in front of the wall of flickering monitors.

"I apologize for becoming agitated," she was saying. "But I insist on finding out why we lost those screen shots. We had a full moon. The trolls were on his tail. We had ideal conditions last night for catching him in the act!"

The hairs on my arms rose. Was she talking about my prince?

I busied myself by sorting through her mail from Friday, removing anything that might be displeasing, while I hung on her every word.

"As soon as Robert gets in Monday morning, tell him I want to see if we can do a digital restoration. We have to at least try. Only Fairyland's entire future is at stake!" With that she slid the phone to Off and tossed it onto her desk blotter, pounding her fist into the armrest of her chair. Even Tinker Bell, snoozing on her pillow, gave a tiny *yip* of alarm.

I remained silent until she finished her tea. When I heard the clatter of the cup on its saucer, I stacked the mail and chirped brightly, "I don't know what you did with your hair this morning, ma'am, but it's even more perfect than usual."

She went, "*Hmph.*"

"No, really. Look." And I brought over her Magic Mirror, so she could see for herself.

"It must be the new rinse I've been using. The one with deadly nightshade." The Queen fingered a few strands. Then, abruptly standing, she said, "Don't think I don't know what you're up to, Zoe. It's no use. We have a huge problem on our hands that's not going to be solved with tea and compliments. Hurry now and get my makeup. The princesses are waiting to be weighed."

I fetched her compact—Alabaster Plaster—and

proceeded to powder her nose. "It's Sunday, ma'am. We don't do weigh-ins on Sunday."

"We do now that Adele has gained three pounds." Sufficiently deathly pale, she ferreted out her lipstick. "Don't argue with me, Zoe. You know how I despise truculence."

Did I ever. After applying a fresh coat of Baneberry Red to her lips, I collected the weight charts, found a new pen, and hurried after the Queen, her robes flowing behind her as she proceeded down the hallway to the elevator to Our World, where three of the second-shift princesses were waiting while Valerie, the gorgeous Sleeping Beauty, was in Wardrobe getting made up.

In their underwear, Snow White, Rapunzel, and Cinderella jumped to attention when we burst through the doors. "All right, ladies. I hope you've been working out and drinking your water." The Queen uncovered the doctor's scale. "I'm sure I don't need to remind you that violation of Rule Number Seven is a deal breaker."

Rule #7: *Princesses will not gain or lose more than three pounds from the recorded weight at their audition.*

Adele, a Cinderella, swallowed hard while Laura, a Snow White, who was as pale as a china doll with hair the color of licorice, stepped onto the scale. She had nothing to worry about, even though she didn't get much exercise lying around all afternoon in a glass coffin. I wrote down her weight: 119.

"Do you know what Rule Number Twenty-Two is, Zoe?" the Queen asked as I charted Laura's weight on the graph in a straight line.

Like a perfect lackey, I parroted it verbatim: "Rule Number Twenty-Two: *Venturing into the Forbidden Zone at any hour and for any reason without written permission from Management will be considered to be an Act Against the Kingdom punishable by automatic exile from Fairyland Kingdom and automatic disqualification from receiving the Dream and Do grant.*"

The Queen graced me with an approving smile. "Very good. Then perhaps you'll understand why I am so upset. Try not to be shocked, my dear, but the trolls have reported that a generic teenage male intern of largely indeterminate identity has been spotted in the FZ."

So my hunch had been right. Her tirade on the phone had been about the prince who'd saved me from the quicksand.

Now what was I going to do?

Miranda, the redhead who'd flown in from Dallas with Ian, was on the scale, waiting. She had the best figure of anyone, and I couldn't understand why she was kept hidden away in Rapunzel's tower.

"One sixteen," the Queen announced. "Not an ounce of deviation. Excellent."

Beaming, Miranda got off and gave Adele an encouraging fist bump.

"I just have to take off my bracelets," Adele said, like that would make a difference.

The Queen heaved a sigh and took me aside, dropping her voice so the princesses couldn't hear. "While we're waiting for Miss Dunkin' Donuts 2013, you should know that when we return to the office, I will need your help in distributing an all-points bulletin informing the interns that one of their own has engaged in the treasonous villainy of sabotage."

"*Sabotage?*" That seemed a tad overboard. "Isn't that kind of extreme? I mean, he was just spotted walking in the woods. What harm is there in that?"

The Queen arched her brow and said, "The harm, Zoe, is in the fact that he blatantly violated Rule Number Twenty-Two, which happens to be a treasonous offense. Unless you know otherwise."

"Uh, no."

She regarded me a half a beat too long for my comfort. "In this proposed all-points bulletin, it shall be noted that any information leading to the apprehension of said traitor shall be immediately rewarded with an elevation in cast status and/or improved odds of winning the Dream and Do. That should serve as sufficient motivation to come forward, eh?"

There it is, Jess's promotion handed to me like Tinker Bell's daily caviar on a silver platter. All I had to do was turn over that shirt swatch, and my cousin would be Cinderella.

I closed my eyes, remembering the sheer panic of slipping deeper and deeper into the sand and how grateful I'd been that the prince had come along at just that moment to catch Tinker Bell and hand me the branch and how I'd sworn that I'd never turn him in.

The Queen swung around to Adele. "Dear girl, what is taking you so long?"

Adele shook her hands nervously. She was blond and blue-eyed like Simone, the other Cinderella who was currently working the park. Unlike Simone, however, Adele tended to be big-boned and athletic—not surprising, considering that during the school year she milked cows on a Wisconsin dairy farm.

"It's just that I didn't expect we'd be weighed this morning and—"

"*Tsk, tsk.*" The Queen cut her off. "There is no vacation from healthy eating!" She rapped the scale with her black fingernail. "Do get on."

My heart went out to poor Adele as she got on the scale. To me she looked fine. More than fine. Healthy. Strong. Wasn't she the model of Cinderella that Fairyland should be promoting, instead of the weak stereotype who had to rely on her elderly fairy godmother for a ride to the ball?

"You do recall the contract you signed to stay the same weight as when you were cast," the Queen said, inching the weights farther to the right.

Adele's yes was barely audible.

"We cannot have one Cinderella who's a size two and another who's a size twelve. It would cause customer confusion. The children should not be able to distinguish you from Simone. Didn't they teach you that in Fairyland summer camp?"

"Yes, ma'am."

"Okay, then." The Queen finally evened out the weights and pursed her lips in dismay. "That's two pounds more, Adele. Unacceptable."

Adele stepped off, tears in the corners of her eyes. "I don't know what's going on."

"Sugar. That's the culprit. I'll tell you what—you won't find me dabbling in that White Death. Why, I haven't touched a single grain or drop since Christmas 1984! It's called discipline, Adele. *D-I-S-C-I-P-L-I-N-E*. Spell it. Learn it. Love it!"

I had to chew my lip to keep from scoffing at the hypocrisy.

The Queen tapped my chart, the one showing Adele's weight going up in a dreaded incline of red ink. "Look at this!"

"I'll try harder," Adele pleaded, not looking.

"Don't try. No one got ahead in the entertainment business by *trying*. *Do!* Remember all the tenets of Wow! and support your sister princesses by making equal sacrifices."

I knocked a pound off Adele's weight and drew the line almost flat. The Queen was too preoccupied with self-righteous lecturing to notice.

Back at her office, I inputted the princesses' weights while the Queen drafted her crazy APB, copies of which I had to insert into everyone's personal mailbox down in Our World.

TO: Fairyland Permanent Staff, Summer Interns,
and Other Assorted Underlings
FROM: Management
RE: Security Alert

It is my unfortunate obligation to inform you that last night our ever-industrious Security Patrols confirmed the sighting of a Teenage Male Intern of Indeterminate Identity crossing into the Forbidden Zone.

As you know, this is a blatant violation of Rule #22, which requires swift punishment. Dangers await in said zone, and we simply cannot risk allowing our summer interns to put themselves in harm's way. (Moreover, our insurance carrier forbids it.)

In addition it is our understanding that said male possessed ulterior motives that violate the Fairyland Code of Ethics.

Therefore, in light of the Direness of this situation and the Expediency with which it needs to be resolved, we, Management, are extending a one-time offer: Any intern with information leading to the apprehension of this traitor will be rewarded with an immediate promotion in cast status. If the informant happens to already be a member of Fairyland royalty (prince, princess), then the reward will be an improved chance of winning the Dream & Do grant that, as you know, currently stands at $25,000.

Pertinent details, tips, and particulars should be written, signed, dated, and, in the interest of preserving confidentiality, deposited in the Customer Feedback box outside Personnel. Any information deemed meritorious will result in a personal meeting with Management.

Your cooperation in this matter is highly appreciated. Thank you.

Sincerely,
Management

That evening I would discover the Queen hadn't been entirely forthright in her memo. Turned out the "Teenage

Male Intern of Indeterminate Identity" wasn't that indeterminate after all. She had an inkling of who he was. . . .

It was the parade, and the Queen and I were side by side on the float that rode behind the dancing princesses and princes. They twirled and bowed, clapped and kissed, in a chaste choreography of the Fairyland theme song: "We Are Family."

Dash was paired as usual with Valerie, a French Caribbean Sleeping Beauty whose complexion was similarly flawless. Her long brown hair fell to her shoulders in natural waves that I, having been born with straight hair, envied with every fiber of my being.

When the Queen wasn't looking, I took a minute to focus on their kiss, searching with forensic scrutiny for signs of genuine affection absent from the other couples who were simply acting their parts, and decided there was more to Dash and Valerie than mere performance. Their lips touched a little too long; his hand held hers a little too tightly. Despite my resolve not to mind, I couldn't help feeling a twinge of disappointment.

"Give it up, Kiefer," Ian said, coming up next to me in his Puss 'n Boots costume. "I told you. Never trust a dude who doesn't eat steak."

I flung a Tootsie Pop at his cat head. He caught it midair and handed it to a boy in shorts. "That's the best you got? Give it another try."

I aimed and fired. Again, Ian lifted his left hand and snatched it without looking. He gave it to a little girl, removing his feathered cap and bowing deeply. She reached up and gave him a kiss on his furry cheek that he accepted with a hand over his heart, stumbling and swooning as if overcome with love.

I laughed, mostly because he was so ridiculous in that costume with its thigh-high boots. "Those boots really work for you."

"You sure?" He twisted and lifted his cape and craned to see his backside. "I worry they make my butt look big."

The Queen cleared her throat in warning that we weren't supposed to be goofing off while on the job. Chastened, I went back to work, tossing candy, catching fruit. But Ian, I noticed, simply gave her a salute and ran into the crowd, completely unperturbed.

The Queen ducked a flying apple that I managed to grab on the first bounce. "Do you know him well, Zoe?" she asked.

"Kind of. He hangs out with another furry, Karl the Wolf."

She studied him a little longer. "Interesting."

"Why?"

She crooked her skeletal finger. "Heaven forfend such intelligence be leaked to the masses, but last week I ordered Security to install a secret camera by the hole in the fence where we suspect our traitor has been egressing. Unfortunately there was a minor malfunction in the power supply, and the images from last night are blurred."

That was why she was throwing such a fit this morning. Her hidden camera had failed. "I'm sorry, but I'm confused." I tossed a handful of Smarties to a group of Girl Scouts. "Why don't you just repair the fence?"

"Oh, no, dear girl. We want to apprehend this violator. *Carpe Sceleratum!* Fortunately the camera has been fixed, and our success is assured. In the interim, from what I could discern by analyzing the albeit murky still shots, our devious delinquent was dark-haired and slim, much like one Ian Davidson when he is not in costume."

Only, it couldn't have been Ian, because the guy who'd rescued me from the quicksand had been a prince using his princely voice and wearing the princely cologne that Wardrobe kept guarded under lock and key. And Ian was the Puss 'n Boots.

Not that I could tell Her Majesty this—unless I wanted to lose my job and doom Jess to a summer of "Oh! What big eyes you have, Grandma!" But I would have to find some way to get the message across before it was too late and Ian was sent back to Texas with a Do Not Return stamp on his forehead.

"With all due respect, ma'am, Ian doesn't seem like the

law-breaking type. I think you might be mistaken."

"Of course you do." She reclined slightly, her eyes reduced to sinister slits. "Be careful, Zoe. The heart is a clever trickster that delights in playing the brain for a fool."

Ten

"You know you've got to find that prince," Jess said, turning off the shower. "You have to warn him that the Queen's out for his head."

This had already occurred to me, too. I switched off the water in my stall and grabbed a towel. "I know, but how? I can't exactly play Prince Charming going from door to door in the Royal Tower with a swatch of black flannel I found on a thornbush looking for some guy with the matching shirt."

"Yeah, but the princes don't spend all their free time in their rooms. I've seen them swimming in the Little Mermaid's Falls after the park closes or playing pickup basketball over at Jack's Beanstalk. Parties? Wardrobe?

The cafeteria? There's got to be some place where they take off their shirts."

I quit toweling to replay what she'd just said. *The cafeteria?* "Is that where RJ hangs out?"

A long, painful sigh echoed in the other stall. "I don't know where RJ hangs out. He says he spends his nights reading in his room and getting ready for Columbia in the fall, but I'm sure that's just an excuse. Do you think he has a girlfriend?"

The ever-impossible question. "How would I know?"

"Because you're good at sensing stuff like that. He claims he doesn't."

"Then he probably doesn't." I collected my shampoo and conditioner and plunked them into my plastic carrier, thinking that guys were never honest about relationships unless they were up against a wall.

"I hope you're right, because I can't tell what he wants. He acts as if he likes me. We meet up for coffee every morning and go for runs and sit really close, but . . ."

"You just want him to make a move."

"Exactly. I've got to take action, or this summer's going to go by without so much as a kiss." Jess wrung out her hair. "Maybe I should ask him if he has any inside information on the Queen and Ian. She's so psycho, you know that once she convinces herself Ian's the traitor there'll be no turning back."

Jess had a point. This was a woman who lectured on the evils of sugar while snarfing down two bars of dark chocolate a week. Talk about the Queen of De-nial. "So you think I should say something to her beyond what I've said about him being innocent?"

"Kind of. I mean, I don't want you to get in trouble, but you have to do the right thing, Zoe, and that's admitting you were in the Forbidden Zone and you talked to this so-called traitor, and it definitely wasn't Ian. Judging from his cologne and British accent, it was a prince."

But was that the right thing? In the eyes of Fairyland Management, it was reporting the "delinquent" who'd violated Rule #22. For Jess, it was giving a heads-up to the stranger who saved me from the quicksand and, for me, it was warning a friend that he was in danger of being wrongly accused of a crime he didn't commit.

I was about to point out my conundrum when the door to the bathroom creaked open, and someone left. I froze. Jess quit talking and waited. Whoever had been there could have heard everything, including that I knew the traitor was not Ian—that he was, in fact, a Prince Charming and that I was about to warn him.

Jess and I simultaneously said, "Crap!"

Despite our panic about the eavesdropper, it seemed we were in the clear. Over the following days, it was business as usual in the front office. No one came forward with information to claim a promotion. There were no more sightings of saboteurs "egressing" from the hole in the fence. For the most part, the memo seemed to have been read by the interns, tossed into recycling, and largely forgotten. Everything was back to normal.

Or, at least, it would have been were it not for two unscheduled real royal VIP visits that sent the Queen into a tizzy.

The first was a Saudi sheik who'd decided on the spur of the moment to visit the park with his three wives and nine kids. They took up the entire penthouse floor of the Fairyland Kingdom Resort, and it was my assignment to reserve facials, manicures, and pedicures at the Fairyland spa for the wives while leading the nine kids around the park in sweltering heat.

Their visit was followed by a certain young British duke and his new wife—whose identities I was sworn never to reveal, though I have to say that when he kissed my hand and complimented me on my "superb bottled-water distribution," I practically fainted.

Because of all this VIP activity, Jess and I didn't get down to hunting for my prince until the following Saturday night, when a group of guys jumped in the Frog Prince's Pond after throwing around the Frisbees on Fiddler's Green.

We were walking Tinker Bell—an automatic pass to be anywhere—and so we *just happened* to be in the Haunted Forest and *just happened* to stop by the pond and inspect a bunch of shirts flung all over the place. We found several tees but nothing in black flannel aside from a black button-down oxford cloth that didn't quite fit the bill, though it was close.

"Did you bring the swatch?" Jess whispered.

"No way. I'm not taking that thing out of its hiding place until I know for sure it's the right shirt."

Jess said, "That's an oxymoron."

"*You're* an oxy-moron."

Turned out, the black oxford-cloth shirt belonged to Marcus.

"Hi, Marcus!" Jess shoved the shirt into my hands.

I mouthed, *Thanks a lot.*

"Hey, what's up?" he asked, toweling water off his six-pack abs. Even in the dim light, I could make out the purple and red bruises from the falls off his horse.

He jutted his chin toward his shirt. "I think that's mine."

"Here," I said, handing it to him. "You dropped this."

"Oh, wow, thanks."

Jess gave me a nudge.

"You two going to the party tonight?" he asked, running a hand through his wet blond hair.

"Can't," I said. "I promised to play a game with Karl." And I could not ditch Karl, whose self-esteem from the Febrezed-puke wolf head was already rock bottom.

Also, the Queen was vehemently opposed to my partying, as she'd made known that very morning when she'd said, "I trust you won't succumb to the temptation of adolescent festivities that periodically arise here, Zoe. Do try to remember that the primary duty of a lady-in-waiting is to be at my beck and call, not rousting about with some hideous testosterone-laden Neanderthals."

And because I was still on probation from the flower-picking incident, I'd said, "Yes, ma'am."

She'd continued to study me warily. "Just so you know, I am not above testing the veracity of your assurance."

Meaning, she would wake me with a bogus errand. "Go ahead. You won't find me having fun."

"I certainly hope not!"

So that's why I had to stay in the dorm. *Ugh.*

Marcus said, "That's too bad. Word is it's gonna be sweet."

"I thought I might go," Jess said shyly, which was news to me. "Though if it's only for princes and princesses . . ."

"No, no. You should definitely come," he said. "In fact, I'll keep an eye out for you."

Jess brightened. "Really?"

"Yeah. It'll be cool."

"All right," said Jess. "Meet you there."

"Awesome."

While we were walking Tinker Bell back to her boudoir, I said, "You do realize he has the IQ of Play-Doh."

Jess shrugged. "That's okay. I like Play-Doh. It's soft and squishy and has so many useful purposes."

I wondered if one was getting RJ to finally make a move.

Eleven

That night I met the outlaw prince again.

On purpose.

Or by accident.

I still wasn't sure.

I was playing The Settlers of Catan with Karl in the rec room like a good little lackey when my iPhone started playing "Every Breath You Take."

It was 10:59, one minute earlier than I'd expected. I pumped my fist. "Called it!"

Karl, who'd bet on midnight, fished out five bucks from his pocket. "No fair. You work for her." He slammed the fiver on the table.

I took it off his hands. "There's gotta be some perks,"

I said, secreting my win into the front of my bra. "Excuse me, will you?" And I took the phone out to the hall.

Thanks to the miracle of FaceTime, the Queen's pale visage filled all four-by-two inches of the screen. Her makeup had been removed, exposing her true features, which were extraordinarily corpselike, and her hair was gone, tucked into what appeared to be a white turban.

But that wasn't what I found shocking. It was her eyeballs.

They were rolling wildly in their sockets.

"Ma'am. Are you okay?"

"I most certainly am not! There is a mote in my eye, Zoe, and I need you here posthaste to remove it."

"Just blink," I said.

"What do you think I've been doing? I've been blinking so much, my eyelids have biceps. Now stop with the dillydallying and hurry. I can't sleep until this cursed offender has been extricated from my ocular perimeter!"

The Queen's verbiage was the perfect example of what my English teacher called using fifty words when one will do.

With apologies to Karl, I went upstairs to the Queen's office, where a door led to her private quarters in a separate turret. Using my master key, I opened the gold lock and stepped into a marble hallway lined with exquisite, thick Persian carpets and beige walls covered in framed photo after framed photo of . . . *her.*

"Hurry, Zoe!" she beckoned from a far room. "I'm in agony!"

"Yes, ma'am." I would have liked to have lingered over what might possibly have been a shot of her with Justin Bieber, but clearly time was of the essence as I scurried past a pair of ornate French doors to her chilly air-conditioned bedroom.

Against one wall was a humongous four-poster bed, and in the center of that, lost among piles of white bedding and white pillows, was a rail-thin figure tossing and turning as if she were on fire.

"Help! I am blinded!"

I rushed to her side and adjusted her bedside lamp but found nothing except for one seriously bloodshot eye. Still, figuring she'd never be satisfied until I removed something, I ran a finger over her lower lashes and faked success.

"All done. See?" I held up my bare finger.

She squinted. "No, I don't. And it still hurts."

"Because you've irritated it. Now lie back and close your eyes," I said, fluffing up a pillow. "And let your natural tears do their job. That's what my mother used to say."

The Queen lay back as I tucked her in. "What else did your mother used to say?"

"That if you can't sleep, try to see how many words you can make from a bigger word."

"Like *incarceration*?"

"I was thinking more along the lines of *petunia* or *lavender*. You know, something pleasant."

"Oh." She seemed disappointed with the floral options but gamely rattled off *pet, pen, pie, pit, tip, tan, tap, nit, nip*. "It's no use. I can't sleep. It's the stress, what with the traitor and those dwarfs giving me such trouble."

Earlier today it had been discovered that Grumpy had fallen in love with Bo Peep and was now as cheerful as one of her lambs while Sleepy had become mildly addicted to energy drinks and seemed bent on singing "Hi, ho!" at warp-speed.

Seriously, everything down at Snow's was all wrong.

"I need my sleeping potion," the Queen declared. "Call Chef and have him concoct a batch. Tell him it's an emergency."

It was almost midnight. I wasn't sure if that was fair to Chef, who was usually in the kitchen by 4:00 a.m.

"Do it!" she croaked.

Chef was on her phone's speed dial, and our conversation took all of a minute, concluding with several choice swears on Chef's part plus, "I'll leave it on my doorstep. Don't wake me again." *Click.*

I hated doing that. "I'll be right back. I just have to go

over to his house and get the stuff."

"He lives far in the Haunted Forest, way behind Hansel and Gretel's Candy Cottage."

There were several employee cottages there that weren't attractions. "No problem. Back in a jiffy," I said, tiptoeing out.

"You can't miss it," she called. "It's the one closest to the Forbidden Zone."

I stopped and smiled to myself, deciding the Queen must have passed me off for an idiot. This emergency was indeed a test, though not to see whether I'd gone to the party.

It was a test to see if I could catch a spy.

Ian was on his way to the party when I ran into him on the fairy path. "Hey, I'll go with you," he said, adding, "unless, um, you're going to meet someone."

I laughed at his lame attempt at subtlety. "Like Dash?"

He shoved his hands in his jeans pockets and kept a brisk pace. "You like him, don't you?"

"He's nice enough. I don't really even know him."

"To know him is to love him. That's the princesses' take, anyway." Ian kicked a stray stone off the path that, due to the old-fashioned gas lamps, glittered even in the dark.

"Well, obviously he's kind to animals, even

cannibalistic chickens, so that raises his hotness right there," I teased.

Ian groaned. "No, you're not going to get me to go that far."

"As if you would."

"Really? You wouldn't believe the lengths I've gone to . . ." He quickly changed the subject. "So you must have the scoop. What's up with that whacked memo the Queen sent out the other day? A traitor? She has to be kidding."

"Or nuts."

"Or nuts," he agreed.

We headed side by side into the Haunted Forest. It was darker there, even with the gas lamps, and more private, for which I was thankful, seeing as how I had to bring up a subject that was probably going to ruin his night. "Look, I've been meaning to talk to you about that." I took a breath. "Oddly enough, you're her prime suspect."

He stopped and turned to me, stunned. "Get out."

"To make a long story short, she had a camera set up by the hole in the fence to the Forbidden Zone. The images she got back were blurry because of a glitch, but they managed to capture a guy who was slim and dark—"

"And tall and sexy?" He kept his expression dead

straight. "Because if he's so hot he broke the camera, then I was definitely the dude." He held up his hands. "Guilty as charged."

Gullible me, I actually wondered if he was serious until his whole face broke into one big grin. "Yeah, I have no idea what she's talking about. I didn't even know there was a hole in the fence. Or that there was a fence. And where's this so-called camera?"

"Wherever it is, you shouldn't go near it, because she got it repaired and now it's working."

"All the more reason, don't you think? That way she can compare and see for herself that it wasn't me." He started heading even deeper into the Haunted Forest, and when we passed Hansel and Gretel's Candy Cottage, its white picket fence glowing strangely, I grew nervous that he just might try something foolish.

"You don't know her, Ian. It'll only confirm her suspicions if you show up on one of those shots."

He let out another laugh like I was overreacting. "Chillax, Zoe. She might be kind of crazy, but she does manage a huge theme park and has for years. There's gotta be some grounding to her."

If only he'd been in her apartment a half hour ago. *Help! I am blinded!*

"The party is that way," I said, when we got to the Witches' Crossing intersection. We could make out the green glow of the Frog Prince's Castle in the distance and even this far away hear the faint *boom, boom, boom* of a pounding bass beat.

"You wanna take a shortcut?" He reached out for my hand as easily as if we'd been friends forever. "We can get there without having to do that unnecessary half-mile loop."

He led me off the sparkling fairy path and through the forest in violation of several rules. My heart fluttered slightly as often happens whenever I'm on the verge of doing something I shouldn't, especially since I knew the Queen was desperately waiting for her potion.

"Um, I really should be heading the other way," I said.

"Worried that the trolls will catch you stepping off the path? Don't be. They're in bed getting their beauty sleep."

"No, it's not that, it . . ."

"Low branch!" He pushed aside a tree limb, and we emerged from the forest into the castle's backyard. Princes and princesses and furries in civilian clothes were dancing in the warm night under the light of tiki torches. Some people were sitting on the fake lily pads dangling their legs in the green-lit water and tossing around a Frisbee. Over in the corner on an oversize red toadstool were Jess and Marcus—making out!

I hoped RJ wasn't there to see this. Or maybe that was the whole idea.

"Looks pretty decent." Ian was still holding my hand. "Wanna go in?"

I wiggled my hand free. "I can't. I have to do an errand for the Queen."

"Now? It's gotta be close to midnight."

"A little after, to be exact."

He cocked his head. "It won't be any fun without you there. Who will I tease?"

I was about to shoot back something about the princesses when I lifted my chin and realized he was looking at me in a funny way, more than just his usual joshing self.

Suddenly my senses sizzled, as if a switch had been flicked and everything was in high-def. For the first time this summer, I detected the faintest whiff of briny air from the sea miles away and became aware of how my arms were damp from the falling dew. The fireflies seemed brighter, and Ian's breathing sounded heavier. I hadn't realized before how tall he was or that I desperately wanted to touch his hair to feel if it was as soft as it looked or that his brow, so determined, shadowed dark, twinkling eyes.

Please tell me I'm not blushing and, if I am, please tell me he can't see that in the dark, I thought as heat shot up the back of my neck. The only way to maintain equilibrium was by concentrating on my bare toes.

Ian gave me a gentle nudge. "Don't be that girl, Zoe. You're allowed to have a life, too, you know. Nothing the Queen wants at midnight can't wait until morning."

Normally I would have agreed. But this was a sleeping potion, and she needed it an hour ago. "I really want to go, Ian. You don't know how much. But . . ."

He put both his hands on my shoulders and bent his head close to mine, nose to nose. It was the closest we'd ever been.

"Okay, I can see you mean it, so I won't be offended that you're blowing me off." He reached into his pocket and pulled out a key chain, taking off a small flashlight. "You should have this for the way back. It doesn't put out a ton of light, but it gets you there."

I curled my fingers around his gift, grateful. "Thanks."

"It's the least I could do. Sure you don't want me to go with you wherever it is you're going?"

"To be honest, she'd kill me if she found out I told anyone else."

"Thought as much." He hesitated, like he wanted to say something else, but then he backed up toward the castle. "Thanks for the walk. And stay away from the Queen's trap, Zoe. I'd hate to see you be sent upriver."

"Would you?"

"You bet."

Too casual to be meaningful and, yet, the way he

lingered suggested that maybe Ian Davidson was beginning to think of me as more than a chicken-loving vegan fool.

I turned and, smiling to myself, ran to find Chef's house while Ian went to the party. The last thing I heard as I ducked into the woods were the princesses screaming his name.

Twelve

I never should have tried to take Ian's shortcut. I always get in trouble when I don't go by the book.

It had seemed so straightforward when he was leading the way—down a gentle hill, left at the rock outcropping, around a pine grove, and voilà! In five minutes I should have been on the path.

But now I had no idea where I was, and with only Ian's small and—*eeep!*—flickering penlight for guidance, I was beginning to worry that I had somehow accidentally wandered into the Forbidden Zone. You could tell the difference because the Haunted Forest was manicured and regularly cleared of underbrush.

This place was wild and overgrown. And buggy.

I scratched my ankles until they were raw. The mosquitoes had sensed my warm human flesh and had descended like a swarm of vampires, ruthlessly feasting on my blood.

Also, flip-flops? What had I been thinking taking the so-called shortcut in those? Please. I did not want to imagine what lay in wait to lunge at my bare feet—timber rattlesnakes. Spiders. Ticks galore.

I brushed off my legs. We'd spent a week in AP bio studying the life cycle of the common deer tick and how you could be bitten and infected with Lyme disease and not know it until a giant bull's-eye bite swelled up on your leg and all your joints started hurting.

I really regretted remembering that.

If I'd chosen the path instead of the shortcut, I'd probably be in bed by now, I thought while scrabbling up a mossy incline, my stupid flip-flops sliding over dead leaves and sticks. I got to the top and almost fainted with relief. A light shone dimly through the trees. Or was it a star? No, it was definitely a light. A *porch* light.

There was a *crash* to my right, deep in the dark part of the forest. A deer, I told myself. New Jersey was lousy with them. Still, I wasn't exactly eager to stick around and make sure, so I started running, flip-flops and all. Running toward that light.

"*Every breath you . . .*"

My heart practically exploded from my chest. Honestly.

I had to change that ringtone. I grabbed the phone from my back pocket and slid it to On.

"Zoe!" the Queen trilled. "Where *are* you?"

"I'm on my way!" I started running again, accidentally stubbing my toe on an exposed tree root. Unspeakable pain rippled up my foot and calf, rendering me speechless.

"Well, hurry up, because there's a scratching sound outside my window that's annoying me. I was almost asleep when it woke me up. Make it stop."

I quit rubbing my aching foot. Hold on. Hold on just a minute.

She was almost asleep?

"Zoe, are you there? I can't see you!"

I held the phone to my face, hoping it adequately reflected the misery she was inflicting. "Can you describe this sound, ma'am? Was it an owl? A dog? A bird?"

"I don't know what kind of animal it was! I'm not a blubbering Boy Scout!"

Oddly enough, that's when I did hear a weird sound—and not the innocent rustling of leaves by some rodent. It was more like a *thwack-thwack-thwack* of footsteps coming through the undergrowth.

"I'll go check it out," I said, turning off the phone before she heard it, too.

I stood quietly listening, my pulse racing, my mind spinning out of control as I imagined every bizarre form of attacker—a wandering loner, a member of a Newark street gang with a poor sense of direction, the legendary New Jersey Devil!

And then logic prevailed. This park was in the middle of the New Jersey Pinelands, a million acres of protected nothingness. Chances were the sounds came from that tick-infected deer or perhaps my prince, in which case I needed to warn him that he was about to be caught in a trap.

"Hello?" I called.

The footsteps stopped, and after what seemed like an eternity, someone responded in that surreal princely voice. "Who's there?"

It was him!

"Don't come any closer," I said. "If I see you and know who you are, I'll have no choice but to report you to the Queen."

There was a pause. "So I guess saving your life was, what, chump change?"

"Please. I've put my ass on the line by not telling her what happened. I promised you I wouldn't tell, and I haven't."

"Thanks. I'd hate to have to explain the *whole* story."

Not that again. "Really, whoever you are, your puns are *pun*-ishment enough."

"What are you doing out here, anyway, Zoe? Isn't it past your bedtime?"

"I could ask you the same thing," I said, trying to get

a bead on how tall he was. Impossible to tell in this darkness. "But we really shouldn't stick around. The Queen's set a trap for you with cameras, one for sure by the hole in the fence."

He said, "Not all of the park is still fenced. They just want you to think it is. One hundred and forty acres is a lot to enclose, and with all the cost-cutting to raise profits, they've let the part no one sees rot into the ground."

I'd been worried about that. "So you mean—"

"You're officially in the Forbidden Zone."

Which officially made me a treasonous criminal, the ultimate poster girl of Fairyland disloyalty. I took a deep breath as my nerves, already rattled, quivered and gave up. "Great. Just great."

He came closer. Again, there was that princely Amazonian cologne. This time I more than swooned. I got positively dizzy.

"Do you want me to show you the way out?" he asked.

"Just tell me."

His directions were simple. Go directly between the two large pines, take about fifty steps straight ahead, and I would be on the path.

It was only then that I noticed the light I'd been running toward was gone.

"I have to ask," I said, when he was done. "What are you doing out here?"

"Hanging in the great outdoors away from the plastic

artificiality of Fairyland. You should try it sometime, Zoe. I especially recommend swimming under the stars in a real pond instead of chemically treated water. Nothing better."

The cologne was indeed intoxicating. My body had started to sway, and my brain was turning fuzzy. I had to pinch my nose to minimize the effects.

I said, "The other day on the phone, the Queen mentioned that because of you, Fairyland's entire future was at stake."

He chuckled softly. "Yeah, right. I don't think so."

A warm breeze rattled the leaves above as he reached out to touch me. "Hey," he said, pulling me toward him. I shut my eyes on the logic that I couldn't report what I couldn't see, right?

He whispered, "Thanks," and I felt his fingers comb through my hair, pushing it back from my cheek. My heart started racing, because I was almost positive he was about to kiss me or something, but we only stood there like that for a while until he said, "I guess this makes us even. I saved your butt; you saved mine."

"Hmmm," was the best I could manage. I was dying to take a peek, but before I could, he'd let go, moving through the woods with the quiet agility of a cougar, leaving me slightly disappointed that I hadn't taken the risk to find out which prince he was.

His footsteps were distant shuffles when I headed

toward the two pine trees and, hopefully, the path. I went about five feet when I was abruptly blinded by a bright lamp.

"Turn that down!" I snapped, trying to shield my eyes.

In front of me stood a stocky figure, hands on hips, hair in a traditional German pageboy, the buckles on his lederhosen visible even through the undergrowth.

Just my luck. A Hansel.

"Well, well, well," he singsonged. "If it isn't the Queen's very own lady-in-waiting caught red-handed conspiring with Fairyland's most-wanted criminal." His headlight zigzagged as he shook his head in condemnation. "And I suppose you're gonna say it was just a coincidence?"

I recognized him as Jake, a somewhat cute Hansel with a big chip on his shoulder, namely his height. Or lack thereof. The other day he'd gone on a rant about how he would have been chosen as a Prince Charming had it not been for one or two missing inches.

"What are you doing out here, Jake?"

"What do you think? You got the memo. Whoever has information about the traitor will automatically be promoted and, therefore, that much closer to getting the Dream and Do." He rubbed his hands together. "I can practically feel that twenty-five thousand dollars burning a hole in my pocket."

"Yes, you'd make a lovely princess." Couldn't resist.

"Very funny, Zoe. If I were you, I'd be worried. I heard what you told him about the cameras, and that Management thinks he's a threat to Fairyland. Do you know what the Queen's going to do to you when she finds out what you said behind her back? That's not exactly showing the Wow! spirit, is it?"

My body went stiff with dread. I knew he'd snitch on me, too. Jake the Hansel was just that ambitious.

"All right, all right. Don't get your lederhosen in a twist," I said, making light. Never let 'em see you sweat. "But how do you know?"

He said, "How do I know what?"

"How do you know I won't get to her first? You need an appointment to talk to the Queen, whereas I, being her closest assistant, could wake her right now if I wanted and tell her that I caught you two conspiring." I took a step closer. "Who's she going to believe? Her most-trusted lady-in-waiting or a bitter little creep whose only chance of advancement is by ratting on his fellow cast members?"

He gasped. That was a Hansel for you—total wimps.

"I can't help it if I'm short," he countered. "You said 'little.' That hurt my feelings."

"Oh, that's too bad. Say, how about a photo of you in the Forbidden Zone to back up my story?"

"We're not allowed to have cameras."

"Correction," I said, turning on the phone that, unbeknownst to him, could only call the Queen and do nothing else. "*You're* not allowed to have a camera."

The phone automatically rang Her Majesty, who got on sounding more irritated than usual. "What is it now, Zoe? Honestly, if you keep pestering me like this, I'll never get the beauty sleep I need."

But by then Jake was long gone.

"Nothing, ma'am. I just want to report that the sound shouldn't be bothering you anymore. Some sort of animal digging, apparently. Scared it off."

"And no sign of . . . *anyone else?*"

I hesitated for a second as I debated how to answer this. "Just a Hansel who was doing a citizen's watch thing on the lookout for your so-called spy."

"Really? Interesting. Now go to bed and quit bothering me. It boggles the mind why you teenagers insist on staying up so late. Might do for you to take a page out of my book. Early to bed, early to rise makes a woman beautiful and wise."

I clicked off the phone and found my way to the path. I never did get that sleeping potion.

Thirteen

"Wake up, sleeping beauty."

Jess's command shattered the peace and warmth of my nice, comfy dream. Hadn't I fallen asleep minutes ago after dragging myself out of bed to walk Tinker Bell? Also, judging from the pitter-patter against the window and the gray skies outside, it was raining. And rain meant sleep.

"It's Sunday," I mumbled. "Leave me alone."

"No can do." Cruelly she stole my pillow and started bouncing on my bed. "Your kind and beneficent boss will soon require your services."

I had to smile. Ever since we'd been overheard in the bathroom gossiping about the prince and the traitor and

Ian, Jess's new tactic was to speak of Fairyland—especially the Queen—in outrageously glorious, insincere terms.

Her theory was that, since the walls in our dorm room were made out of toilet paper and spit, anyone could eavesdrop on our conversations. And with every cast member competing for the Dream & Do grant, you couldn't afford to be caught committing any innocent act of disloyalty.

"Yes," I agreed. "She is so generous." *Generous* being our code word for *hideous*.

"So very generous." Jess stifled a laugh and poked my back. "Now roll over and get your caffeine fix. I have some incredibly juicy gossip from last night."

Jess handed me an Iced Caramel Vanilla Mocha Cappuccino from the cafeteria in Our World, all vanilla soy milk and sugar. Her maroon Bridgewater-Raritan Panthers hoodie couldn't quite cover the purple hickey on her neck.

Class.

She took a sip of coffee. "If anyone asks, I came back from the party early. I definitely did not spend the night in Marcus's room and sneak out just before dawn. Unless it's RJ doing the asking, in which case you might want to suggest that apparently other guys do find me hot."

Oh, no, she didn't. Oh! No! She! Didn't!

Throwing off the sheet, I grabbed my shower caddy and towel. "To the Bat Room. Stat!"

Once we were in the hall, I took my judgment-challenged cousin aside and cornered her by the fire extinguisher in the stairwell, where we were clear of the other dorm rooms. "Tell me you didn't go back to Marcus's room."

"All right. I didn't go back to Marcus's room."

"You didn't?"

"No. I did. But you told me not to tell you that."

Grrrr. Rule #6 specifically stated that boys and girls were *not* allowed in each other's rooms after 10:00 p.m. And it had been *waaaaaaay* past 10:00 p.m. when Jess went back to Marcus's. The party didn't even get going until around eleven.

"Nothing happened," she said.

"Sure." I took another glance at the purple mark and shook my head in utter disbelief. "What if RJ sees that?"

Jess pulled up her sweatshirt. "What if he does?" Her lower lip protruded. "Honestly, Zoe, I'm ready to give up. I've tried everything with this dude—being super nice, laughing at all his jokes, practically sitting on his lap while we watch movies—and nada. I'm beginning to think he really is gay and is just too inhibited to let people know. So here's the test: If he's fine with me and Marcus, if he wants to rehash all the gory details of last night like a friend . . ."

A female troll passed by, hands behind her back on her daily inspection. I said cheerfully, "Good morning on this rainy Sunday, fair Security Person," but she just scowled.

". . . then I'll know it's hopeless," Jess concluded. "You get my point, right?"

"Sure, and I also think that when it comes to guys, you sometimes make things way too complicated than they have to be," I said. "Come on. I've gotta get ready for work."

Because it was before seven on a Sunday morning, our bathroom was delightfully empty, still reeking of the bleach-and-antiseptic spray the cleaning crew had used during the night. I stepped into the shower while Jess served as lookout so we could talk. The bathroom, with its insulating tile and running water, was the safest place to gossip—as long as no one else was in one of the stalls listening in.

"So what did you do while I was at the party?" Jess asked.

I told her about being summoned to remove a mote from the Queen's eye and then her bogus request for a sleeping potion from Chef, who just happened to live on the edge of the Forbidden Zone, and then about running into the prince again and being surprised by Jake the Hansel who'd heard everything.

The only part I left out was the walk with Ian, since

it would have opened up a whole can of worms I wasn't ready to deal with. Jess knew I'd promised my grief counselor that I'd swear off boys for the summer. It was one of the few promises I'd made that, after last night, I desperately wanted to break.

"What do you think he's gonna do?" Jess asked.

My mind was still on Ian, so I said, "Who?"

"Jake the Hansel. Do you think he's gonna go to the Queen like he said, or was he just bluffing?"

I flipped off the shower and wrapped my hair in a towel. "I think he's gonna try. More likely he'll write a letter to her and put it in the Box of Whine outside Personnel like she'd instructed in her memo. That way no one will know who's ratting on who."

Half dressed, I stepped out of the shower soapy clean.

"But you get to go through the box first, right?" Jess craned her neck to check her hickey in the mirror.

"Not lately." I went over to the sink to brush my teeth. "After that memo, the Queen took it over. I don't think she trusts me." I rinsed and spit. "I'll tell you what, if Jake writes that he saw me in the Forbidden Zone last night talking to a prince, I am cooked. She will fire me on the spot, no questions asked."

There was a cough on the other side of the vanity and then the sound of water being turned on. We were not alone.

Again?

I shook my fist at Jess, since she was supposed to have kept an eye out.

"I did. I looked under all the stall doors and everything," Jess whispered. "I don't know where she came from."

I poked my head around to the other set of sinks and found Adele the weight-challenged Cinderella flossing her teeth.

I said, "Hi." *Um, what are you doing here in our second-class bathroom?*

"Don't mind me." She tossed the floss in the trash. "I was too focused on my own stuff to listen to you guys rehashing last night."

Under her breath, Jess went, "Yeah, right."

Adele's pale blue eyes were red-rimmed, like she'd been crying.

"You okay?"

"Never better." In the mirror she flashed me the official Fairyland Kingdom Princess Smile—lots of white teeth touching top to bottom, the way no real person does. "I mean, what could be wrong, right? I'm Cinderella at the most magical place on earth. Wow!"

I watched as Adele smeared on lip gloss and took a haphazard approach to brushing her hair, all the while sniffling and batting her eyes. Guess that's why she was slumming in our neck of the woods—so that her fellow princesses wouldn't see her upset.

"Hey, Adele," I said as she headed out, "I heard you playing your guitar on Humpty Dumpty's Wall the other day, and it was great. What was the song?"

She stopped at the door. "Not anything you've ever heard before. I wrote it."

"You *wrote* it?" That was impressive. "That deserves a legit wow."

This time Adele gave me a real smile. "Thanks, Zoe. You'd be all right . . . if you didn't work for *her.*"

I knew what she was getting at. "It's not my idea to weigh the princesses constantly."

"Yeah, but you're the one who writes us up and charts each little ounce."

I was sorry I'd decided to defend myself, because her mood had quickly soured. "It might be unfair, but that's how I think of you, Zoe, as the proverbial messenger everyone wants to shoot."

I had no idea that was how people felt about me. *Everyone?* I was so shocked that as she flashed one final, triumphant sneer and left, I had to lean against the cold wall to recover.

"Don't listen to her," Jess said, coming up and giving me a hug. "She's just bitter because she knows she's on thin ice with the Queen, and so she's taking out her anger on you. You're awesome."

It was nice for Jess to say. Unfortunately I suspected Adele's dig that I was nothing more than the Queen's henchwoman was truer than my loyal and loving cousin would dare admit. It was quite possible that the other cast members really did secretly despise me just as they despised my boss.

Perhaps rightly so.

I shouldn't have stopped for a quick breakfast—half a banana, a bite of toast, and a cup of regular non-Jess coffee—because in my effort to not starve, I was slightly behind schedule when I arrived with the Queen's breakfast and papers.

"You're late!" she snapped as soon as I pushed open the door. "Put down the tray and come over here. I have a new assignment for you, Zoe, and please don't prevaricate. Be quick on your toes."

Her Majesty was on another tear, pacing back and forth in the control room, grumbling, her arms crossed, while Andy the Summer Cast Coordinator alternately pleaded with her to listen to reason and tried not to trip on her train. At least she'd restored her makeup so that she didn't look so much like a corpse as like a corpse with arched jet-black eyebrows and raw lips.

I did as commanded and put the tray on the wheeled

dolly next to her glass desk. Then I stood waiting. The Queen stopped pacing.

"Curtsy!" she commanded.

Really? Now she was making me curtsy, too?

"Come on. Hop to. We have a lot to do today."

I slid my right foot behind my left, held out the skirt of my dress, bent my knees, and bowed, imitating how the princesses did it during the parade.

The Queen sniffed. "Twirl."

I had no idea where we were going with this, but I held out my arms anyway and, à la Julie Andrews on a mountaintop, spun around crazily, banging once into the watercooler.

"Not like a runaway weed whacker! Twirl like a princess."

Oh, no. She couldn't be thinking . . .

"Twirl!"

So I twirled, hands clasped in front of me in standard Fairyland style.

"She's not perfect, by any means," Andy said. "But she'll do in a pinch."

"She's abominable. A yeti in stilettos would be more convincing." The Queen clapped twice for me to stop.

I stopped and reached for the desk to keep the world from spinning. Twirling and Jess's over-sugared coffee were not a great combination. Pouring myself into the chair, I said simply, "Why?"

"Rise! I did not give you permission to sit."

I jumped up while the Queen sat and applied her signature to a letter Evelyn, her secretary, had delivered on official Fairyland stationery. "Zoe, I need you to serve as a temporary stopgap while I engage in a bit of cast reshuffling. If I bring up a girl from Ordinary to sub for Adele, she'll only get her hopes up."

Sub for Adele? So that explained why Adele was in our bathroom crying, because she'd been canned—already. "Tell me she's not being fired for gaining five pounds."

The Queen folded the letter and shoved it in the envelope. "I will tell you no such thing. I do not discuss personnel matters with interns, even if you are my assistant. Rule Number Fifty-Four-A." She sealed the envelope by pressing her ring into a glob of black wax. "I will, however, inform you that from now on Adele is an Ordinary Cast Member Class B. To wit, a Character Yet to Be Determined."

I chewed a nail, fretting that now Adele probably blamed me for her getting fired.

The Queen regarded me sharply. "Take that finger out of your mouth, Zoe Kiefer. Nail biting is a disgusting habit for the insecure and feebleminded."

Or not, I thought, hiding my hand behind my back so I wouldn't be tempted.

Sudden movement on monitor #24 caught my attention. It was the display for the camera by Personnel, and it also captured the Box of Whine, where I saw one Jake the Hansel approach clutching something to his chest. He checked over his shoulder once, twice, went on tiptoe, and shoved a letter into the box. Then, tidying his blond pageboy wig and straightening his lederhosen, he marched swiftly away from the camera.

That fink!

There was a knock at the door, and Evelyn bustled in with another letter. The Queen read it, sighed, and said to Andy, "Call Norbert Atkinson, our lawyer. I want to make sure he reviews this before I have Zoe deliver it to Marcus Blaisdel informing him of violating the Fairyland rules."

I felt the blood drain from my face. If Marcus was in trouble for bringing a girl to his room, then my cousin was in trouble, too.

"Why do we need to call in a lawyer when that's only a summons for Marcus to come to your office?" Andy asked.

The Queen closed her eyes and flared her nostrils. Andy should have learned, as I had, that she did not appreciate *truculence.* "Please. Just do as I say and . . . don't . . . argue!"

Without another word, Andy took the letter, opened the door, and left so I was alone with the Queen in one of her most foul moods. She pinched the bridge of her nose and whispered, "Sustenance."

I quickly poured a cup of tea and handed it to her. After she took a sip, she replaced it in the saucer and said, "Zoe, I am cursed by the company of dunderheads."

Join the club. "Yes, ma'am." I fixed her a nonfat yogurt and raspberries, chiding myself for not having brought more honey.

"I don't know what I'd do if it weren't for you."

A compliment? That was unexpected. And worrisome. Handing her the delicate china dish, the berries arranged in a uniform pattern of threes as she preferred, I said, "Ma'am?"

The Queen smiled thinly. "You are the only one who executes my orders as I direct with no useless backtalk." She sliced a raspberry in half and nibbled half of that. "You keep Tinker Bell on schedule with regular vigorous exercise." She gave her dog, snoozing on her satin pillow, a gentle pet. "The other day you prevented Sleepy from drinking that awful Five-Hour Energy. You noticed that birds were making a nest in Rapunzel's braid and that the porridge in the Bears' cottage had grown moldy, thereby sparing Goldilocks from all sorts of untold ills. And then, of course, you came to my aid last night."

Okay, this was way too much praise. "Thank you," I said. "I think."

"Which is why I'm all the more disappointed that,

being a close acquaintance of this scoundrel, you did not divulge the nefarious tendencies of one Marcus Blaisdel." She pushed aside her yogurt and sighed. "He may seem like the village idiot, but I'll have to let him go, Zoe. I have no choice. Such behavior as that which our security cameras detected last night cannot be tolerated."

I swallowed. Jess! How had she allowed herself to be caught going in and out of the boys' dorm when she knew that, for safety reasons, a security camera was aimed at the front door?

The only thing I could think to say was, "Ma'am. I have no idea what you're talking about."

"You know," she said, resting her pointed chin on her thin, white hand. "I believe you. By the way, never end a sentence with a preposition such as *about*, Zoe. It is so very pedestrian."

How could she criticize my grammar at a time like this? What was going on?

"All clear!" Andy reappeared, waving the letter. "Norbert says it's fine. However, he asks that you not speak to Marcus in person without making sure you have legal counsel present." He laid the letter on the desk. I read it upside down:

SUMMONS TO ANSWER ALLEGED VIOLATION OF
FAIRYLAND KINGDOM RULE #22:
Venturing into the Forbidden Zone at any hour and

for any reason without written permission from
Management will be considered to be an Act Against
the Kingdom punishable by automatic exile from
Fairyland Kingdom and automatic disqualification
from the Dream & Do grant.

I gasped. "*Marcus* is the traitor?"

This didn't make sense. The prince had caught Tinker Bell and saved me by using a branch to get me out of the quicksand. And then there was his analysis of costs and profits as reasons why Fairyland let much of the fence to the Forbidden Zone decay in disrepair.

Marcus wasn't smart enough to be the traitor.

Unless he'd been holding out on us. Maybe that laid-back surfer persona he had going was a ruse. No, something was off.

The Queen whipped out a pen and applied her signature with a flourish. "Indeed. We have caught our spy. A reliable informant has come forward with damning evidence proving beyond a reasonable doubt that Marcus Blaisdel crossed from the Haunted Forest into the Forbidden Zone at eleven fifty-nine last night."

Uh, no way. He was with Jess. Though I couldn't exactly point this out to the Queen, not unless I wanted my cousin to automatically lose out on twenty-five thousand dollars for going up to a boy's room after ten.

"He's blond, though," I said, wildly fishing. "You said

the security cameras picked up someone who was slim and dark."

"I also said those cameras malfunctioned." The Queen folded the letter, stuffed it in the envelope, sealed it, and handed both to me. "Deliver these to Marcus and Adele. See that they read them while you wait. Then go to Wardrobe. Do me proud as Cinderella this afternoon, Zoe, and you just might end up as a princess for the remainder of the summer."

This was all wrong. Marcus was being unfairly accused of spying, Adele had been fired for five stupid pounds, and Jess would be heartbroken when she saw that the Queen had made me Cinderella and not her.

And, worst of all, I was powerless to save any of them.

Fourteen

The rain had stopped, and the grounds crew was wiping off the benches and the rides to dry everything by opening in a half hour. As I was on my way to delivering Marcus's and Adele's summonses of doom, I tried to cheer myself up by thinking how happy all the little kids on their way to Fairyland would be now that the sun was out. One more reminder why it was important to keep positive and remember that this internship was the coolest of summer jobs—even if my boss was crazy.

I crossed the soggy Fiddler's Green on my way to the boys' dorm and, at its top floor, the Princes' Tower, where Marcus was likely still fast asleep. I was about to wave to Humpty Dumpty sitting on his wall and eating a breakfast burrito when I caught sight of Ian headed my way in his thigh-high boots.

His wavy black hair blew back in the morning breeze as his green cape whipped behind him. Were it not for the cat head under his arm, he'd have easily been mistaken for a prince.

"Ah, I see you survived okay," he said, greeting me with a wide grin.

After our walk the night before, it felt like we were sharing a secret joke—and were simply waiting for the punch line so we could finally laugh.

"I guess I managed to avoid being attacked by fierce wild beasts, thanks to your trusty penlight."

"That penlight's gotten me out of many a tight spot. I still think you should have come with me to the party."

I kept walking toward the dorms. "Yeah, how was it?"

"Awesome, if you're into listening to princesses debate the virtues of Vaselining your teeth for faster smiles. Otherwise . . . pretty boring." He leaned toward me. "It would have been much more fun with you there."

This time, in the broad light of day, I was unable to hide my blush, and Ian must have noticed, because he smiled and said, "So there's hope."

"For what?"

He shrugged, his long legs taking lengthy strides. "We'll see."

"You're weird, you know that?" I was careful to keep my head down out of fear that if I looked into his eyes, I might give myself away. "Where are you off to, anyway? You usually don't do the morning shift."

I winced, since that showed I'd been following his schedule like I was crushing. Which I might have been.

"Are you keeping track of my whereabouts?"

"I'm the Queen's assistant. It's my job." *As if.*

"Then you probably know that my days of running around the park as a semipsychopathic feline with narcissistic personality tendencies have come to an end." We stopped at the entrance to the boys' dorm.

"What do you mean?"

"You're looking at the newest Prince Charming." He gave a low bow.

I dropped my jaw. "How did this happen?"

"Can't tell you." He zipped his lips. "However, I will say you played a part. After you told me that I was a suspected traitor, I went to the Queen, and we talked and"—he shrugged—"she promoted me to prince!"

So *he* was the informant!

At that moment every positive thought about Ian vanished. I could feel my heart break under the realization that he had lied about another cast member in order to get a promotion that would make him eligible for the Dream & Do grant. He was no better than the grasping, ambitious types like Jake the Hansel. Actually he was worse. At least Jake the Hansel reported something he'd seen and overheard.

Ian couldn't have seen or overheard anything. He'd been with *me* at 11:59 the night before, thereby making it impossible for him to have caught Marcus in the Forbidden Zone when the Queen said the snitch reportedly saw him.

I was so pissed, so outraged that he could have used me in his scheme, that it was all I could do to keep from wiping that perpetual grin off his face with a good, hard slap.

"Psychopath is right," I snapped. "Thanks to you, Marcus is being kicked out of the program."

Ian's face fell. "The Queen didn't say she would do that."

"You read the memo. What did you think would happen?" I jammed my master key into the boys' dorm lock, fumbling a bit because the key didn't quite fit.

Ian leaned over and opened the door for me with his swipe card. "Here."

I can't believe how wrong I've been about him, I thought as I yanked open the door and swung around so hard, my pearl tiara nearly flew off. "I hope it's worth it, Ian. From every fairy tale I've read, there's a seriously heavy price to pay—when you sell your soul."

* * *

I had to take a few minutes in the stairwell of the boys' dorm to get my act together. I could not let my summer be ruined by a jerk like Ian Davidson, and I shouldn't beat myself up for being fooled by a dark-haired, sweet-talking boy with laughing half-moon eyes. I wasn't the first girl to fall for a guy just because he was Abercrombie hot, and I wouldn't be the last.

Chalk it up to experience and moveon.org.

Right.

I gathered my strength and forced myself to get back to doing my job—as unpleasant as it currently was.

Even though this was my umpteenth trip to the Princes' Tower—most often to wake Marcus—I was still struck by the luxuriousness of these dorms compared to the Ordinary Cast Members digs one floor below. There, the hallways were narrow and stank of sweaty armpits and pitted-out sneakers, the time-worn walls covered with graffiti concerning unfavorable attributes of Rumpelstiltskin.

Here in the princes' quarters, everything was plush, with thick blue carpeting and crystal chandeliers. If you ask me, it was almost too ritzy for a bunch of seventeen-year-old boys.

And yet I couldn't help thinking that behind one of these doors was the real traitor—I mean, the real Prince

Charming—who'd saved me twice, if his directions last night out of the Forbidden Zone counted as a form of rescue, too.

All I had to do was use the master key to open each room and find that shirt, and I'd know for sure. The answer was practically inches away.

The hall was deathly quiet, the princes either working in the park or working out in the gym. My palms itched as I fingered the key that was begging to be used. I might have resisted its temptation if the first door I saw hadn't been marked: Dash Merrill.

Here's what was odd: Orientation aside, Dash and I hardly spoke except when we bumped into each other at the salad bar. Mostly he acted like I didn't exist. He was either off with Valerie or hanging with his prince bros. I used to think he was just stuck-up, but if he were the real prince and careful about his connections, perhaps he was keeping his distance to protect me.

I put my ear to the door. Nothing. Dash usually did the first shift with Valerie, so it was a safe bet that I could search his stuff with impunity. Anyway, if I happened to be caught, I had a ready excuse: I was trying to find Marcus and had somehow ended up in the wrong room. *Completely understandable.*

Quietly I removed my key and placed it in the lock, snapping it open easily. With one last check down the hall, I stepped inside and closed the door silently.

The room was surprisingly messy for such a well-kept guy. I picked through the heap of clothes on the floor, avoiding several pairs of plaid boxers. Under the boxers were books, and under the books were jeans, and under the jeans were more books, and under them, shirts. I was like an archaeologist digging through teenage-male debris in search of the holy grail: one very Seattleish black flannel shirt.

Nothing there, I knelt to search under the bed, since it made sense that a person in such a precarious position would try to hide the evidence. As far as I could tell, there were several dust bunnies but no shirt.

Had he hidden it in his luggage? I walked over to the closet for a look-see.

Sure enough, there was a dark-green backpack. I thrust my arm deep inside and rustled around. Contact case. (He wore glasses?) A bottle of leaking sunscreen. Ick! And . . .

"Can I help you?"

Crap. *Trolls!*

I yanked my hand out of the backpack, wiped the sunscreen on my dress, and came out of the closet to find none other than Dash Merrill himself recently returned from the shower, dripping wet, with only a rather small white towel wrapped around his hips.

Gentle Reader: I have not led a sheltered life. I'm a frequent beachgoer, and I've seen plenty of guys with their shirts off. And some I'd literally pay good money to put their shirts on. Dash did not fall into that latter category, because he was Dash Merrill and his body was amazing. Smooth chest. Impressive shoulders. Muscular in a natural, i.e., not weird iron-pumping way.

"Hi!" I held up my hand dripping with white sunblock, mortification seeping through my pores.

I realized then that "looking for Marcus" wasn't going to cut it, as it was very rare to find normal high school seniors, even those of questionable intelligence, hanging out in their friends' backpacks. In their closets.

Dash closed the door behind him. "You mind, uh, explaining what's going on?"

"What?" I said innocently.

He pointed to the closet. "You going through my pack."

"Was I going through your pack?" I conjured a dismissive chuckle. "No, no. Hardly. The Queen asked me to do a spot-check for illicit food." I dropped my voice and cupped my mouth in confidentiality. "Apparently we have a bit of a *problemus rodentis*."

He wasn't buying my ruse. "Shouldn't that be Maintenance's thing?"

"It will be, if we find the mice."

"I thought you just said there's a rodent problem."

"An *alleged* rodent problem. You have to stay on top of these things, you know, if you don't want to be infested with rats."

Dash tossed his black Dopp kit on the bed. "Gee," he said, keeping a tight clutch on that towel. "And here I thought you were searching for something else."

I swallowed hard. Was he implying what I thought he was implying? "Nope. Just food, other than, of course, Marcus."

"Marcus?" He raised an eyebrow. "In my closet?"

"Or thereabouts." The trick was to keep your tone calm and even.

"Marcus isn't here. He's down in Wardrobe getting his coat altered. If you hold on a minute, I'll take you there."

I started to say that wasn't necessary, since I went to Wardrobe twice a day and obviously knew the territory, but Dash insisted. "If you wouldn't mind turning your head . . ."

Had I been staring? Oh my. Red-faced, I stepped inside the closet again and closed the door while outside, inches away, Dash slipped into one of those boxers I'd probably touched. Seconds later he opened the closet wearing a gray tee and jeans. He put his finger to his lips, like I wasn't supposed to talk.

"Come on," he said loudly. "I'll take you to Marcus."

I followed him dumbly down the hall, my mind reeling in confusion. We walked through the doors and past a security troll to the elevator that would take us directly to Our World. We got in. Went down one floor, and the elevator lurched to a stop.

Dash had pushed the emergency button and taken off his shirt, throwing it over the small camera in the corner. Monitor #21, I believed. Not that, you know, I spent too much time staring at the camera in the elevator to the Princes' Tower. Ahem.

"I'll make this quick," he said, looking down at me with a kind of longing that I found half intriguing, half freaky. But mostly intriguing. "I want to thank you for last night. You really saved me with that heads-up."

Holy . . . ! I was gobsmacked. *Dash was my prince?* I'd been right? "So it *was* you?"

He grinned sheepishly, busted. "I don't want to bring you into this any more than I have to. I just need to know you're not going to tell . . ." He cocked his head toward the camera. "She's monitoring my every move these days, so I think she's on to me."

"I'm not going to tell, and by the way, she thinks Marcus is you." I showed him the letter. "And he's being fired for it."

Dash set his jaw and cursed. "That sucks. He didn't do anything wrong."

"Aside from showing up late every day for work, true.

Also, I think even Lulu refuses to let him ride her. I think she's insulted that he keeps falling off."

I counted the seconds in my head. How long until the trolls came to start up the elevator? How long until the Queen observed that the camera had been grayed out by a Fruit of the Loom?

"There's something else," I added. "Jake the Hansel caught me after you left. And this morning I saw him slip a sealed envelope into the Box of Whine. I'm sure it details everything I said to you."

"We need to get that, then."

Well, duh. "We also need to get this elevator moving and the T-shirt back on your body. The Queen's probably already radioed the trolls to investigate."

"Don't worry. One step ahead of you." He punched the Restart button, and the elevator began to move. But he made no effort to get his shirt.

"This might seem kind of forward," he said, coming closer, "but I think it's the only way to throw them off." Then he leaned down, paused for a second, and brought his lips to mine.

What? My eyelids flew wide open in shock.

He stepped back and grinned. "Okay?"

More than okay. Actually really nice. I smiled as the elevator doors flew open to two awaiting trolls. Dash swept his lips over mine again, only kissing me deeper. I did my part by throwing my arms around his bare neck. In the process I accidentally took a big whiff of that princely cologne.

Suddenly I became fixated on the softness of his mouth, the feel of his wet hair, how even the sound of us kissing sent me into a tailspin.

"Excuse us," one of the trolls said gruffly. "You two coming out, or you gonna stay in there all day?"

Dash released me from his clutches, and I gasped for breath, my body weak and wobbly.

"My apologies, gentlemen," he said, grabbing his shirt and pulling me through the trolls. "You know how young love is."

He said *young love*!

The trolls snickered like they knew. Oh, boy, did they know. I had to bite back giggles of my own as the cologne's effects gradually wore off and I became, again, fully functioning.

"Sorry about that," Dash said, once we'd turned the corner to the hallway that led to the Box of Whine outside Personnel. "There didn't seem like any other option."

"It was fine." I blinked away the fuzzy filter that made everything glow. "I, um, enjoyed your logic."

"You're all right, Kiefer. Now let's go find the Hansel's letter."

The Box of Whine was a large, wooden box nailed to the wall outside Personnel. Since it was Sunday, Personnel was closed and the hallway vacant. We checked behind us. Dash threw his shirt over the camera again, and I opened the box with my master key. It was empty.

Dash peered in. "That's not good."

"Not good at all." I closed the lid and locked it, trying to think what could have happened. "The Hansel must have given her a heads-up. She never gets her complaints this early."

"Can't you get the complaints before she does?"

"I could. . . . Unfortunately I was supposed to have delivered these letters to Marcus and Adele already."

"Adele too?"

I drew a finger across my throat. "It might read Fairyland on the gates, but there's no promise of happily ever after in this place. You know what the Queen told me the other day? That already half of the interns had disqualified themselves for one reason or another from the Dream and Do grant."

Dash leaned against the wall and ran a hand through his damp hair. "I suppose she didn't say who."

"Nope. Anyway, I've got to deliver these summonses before the Queen has my head, and if you think that's a metaphor, you don't know my boss."

"Anything I can do?" he asked as I headed toward Wardrobe.

"Oh, sure. Just find the troll with the complaints,

knock him to the ground, get the Hansel letter, and give it to me by the end of the day. All without getting caught. No problem, right?"

"No problem."

I'd meant it as a joke, of course. But apparently Dash was the type to take things literally.

Fifteen

After Dash left I went to Wardrobe to deliver my summons to Marcus, quite possibly the suckiest five minutes of my life.

I handed him the sparkling green envelope. "Look, before you open this, I want you to know that I'm going to do whatever I can to clear your name."

Marcus had recently come from Makeup, so he looked nothing like his usual surfer-dude self. His blond hair had been hidden underneath a Prince Charming black hair helmet that magically transformed anyone who wore it into a living Ken doll, and his eyes were huge in scary eyeliner.

He slid his finger under the Queen's seal and removed

the letter, his blue eyes zigzagging from side to side. I watched in dread as the news sank in. "You mean, I'm being fired?"

"I don't know." *Prosecuted, more like it.* "You have to go see her."

Then those baby blues turned cold. "This is about Jess last night, isn't it?"

"No. Definitely not." I crossed my chest. "The Queen doesn't even know."

"You told her, didn't you?"

"Marcus, I said not a word. You have to trust me on this." My heart started beating fast. I couldn't stand it when people started hating on me for no reason. I don't know, call me human.

Trish the stylist came down the hall, two pairs of glasses hanging around her neck. "Oh, Zoe. I'm so glad you're here. I just got messaged from the front office about the change in casting and was trying to find you. We'll need to take your measurements and do the necessary alterations to Adele's costume, so you'll be ready this afternoon to go on as Cinderella."

Marcus glared. He might have had the IQ of earwax, but he was smart enough to figure out that I was moving up, and he and Adele were moving down.

"Oh, I get how it is. You rat on your cousin and me and—wham!—you get bumped up to Cinderella." He crumpled the summons into a ball. "You know, I was worried about you telling the Queen, but Jess said you were chill. Wait until she hears about this." He tossed the summons ball onto the floor and brushed past me, rudely bumping his shoulder against mine.

That was so unfair. "You're wrong, Blaisdel. Dead wrong!" I shouted, though it was too late. Marcus was in the elevator, arms folded. He flipped me the bird, and then the doors closed.

I knew I would never see him again.

"This is going well," I said to no one in particular, and went to find Adele.

As I trotted through the maze of the Our World hallways, I tried not to imagine how pissed Jess would be when she learned about Marcus getting fired. Or how disappointed she'd be when he falsely accused me of selling out or what would happen when word got around Our World that I was made Cinderella after I snitched on my own best friend and cousin.

I decided then that you could not pit a bunch of ambitious, talented, extremely theatrical rising high school seniors against one another with twenty-five thousand dollars at stake and not expect blood to be shed. Many of us were going to fall. Maybe even me. Maybe even Jess.

I found Adele in the gym, working out with the rest of the second-shift princesses—Miranda, the redheaded

Rapunzel; Laura, the raven-haired Snow White; and Valerie, the brunette Sleeping Beauty and Dash's possible girlfriend.

This day just kept getting better and better.

Miranda, Laura, and Valerie were blessed with the perfect sort of symmetrical bone structure that made geneticists clap their petri dishes in glee. Miranda had sparkling green eyes and delicate features that called to mind well-bred, long-haired dachshunds. Laura's jet-black hair and alabaster-white skin fulfilled every goth boy's dream. But Valerie, with her exotic looks, was in a different category altogether.

On the opposite end of the spectrum was blond Adele, good ol' Adele, who was huffing and puffing on the cross trainer in her pink spandex, desperately trying to lose the weight that had already stamped her DOA. Watching her try so hard and remembering how she'd been sobbing in the bathroom made me wish the Queen had read the Hansel's complaint and put me on the bus back to Bridgewater first thing in the morning. Anything but this.

"Excuse me, Adele," I whispered, trying to be discreet. "Could I speak to you alone?"

Laura and Valerie, who were lifting weights, exchanged knowing glances in the floor-to-ceiling mirror, but Adele just kept on chugging. She took a swig of water, wiped sweat off her forehead, and refused to make eye contact.

"I've got fifteen more minutes. Can it wait?"

I didn't want to display the summons in all its sparkling Fairyland glory, not with Laura and Valerie hanging on my every word. However, I couldn't keep the Queen waiting a second longer. "Actually it's kind of important." Getting on tiptoe, I put my lips to her ear, "I have something from the Queen."

Adele said, "Yeah. I guessed, seeing as how you're her weasel assistant." Still, she wouldn't get off.

By now Miranda was on the case, too, the three other princesses shooting worried glances at Adele, who was upping the awkward by being so stubborn. Left with no other choice, I pulled out the summons and said, "The Queen wants me to be sure that you read this." When she showed no indication of taking it, I slipped it onto the little shelf where you're supposed to put magazines or your iPod.

"No, thanks." Adele flicked it off. Just like that. It went *pffft* across the room, hitting a treadmill and falling to the floor.

This was like babysitting Jaden Conroy, who used to dump his milk on the table intentionally. Patiently I picked up the letter right as my iPhone sang "Every Breath You Take" . . . in the pocket of my gown.

My boss's pinched face filled the tiny screen. "Where's Adele? Marcus has already come and gone. The second shift starts at two, and she's not here."

Adele kept pumping.

"I'm sorry, ma'am," I said, taking the phone into the hall. "She won't read the summons."

"She won't, eh?" The Queen's crimson lips pursed. "Then put her on. Now."

Oh, god. Please let this be over. I made another trip to the gym, where Adele had taken the cross trainer to its maximum level, her face beet red and glistening with perspiration. "The Queen wants to talk to you." I held up the phone.

Adele snatched it, breathing perhaps more heavily than was necessary, and put it on the book ledge. "I can't read the letter now. I'm on the cross trainer."

"Well, stop that and come here immediately. I need to speak with you."

"No can do. I need to lose seven pounds by Monday, remember?"

"Not necessary. You're a Class B Ordinary Cast Member, mostly like a Fairy Godmother now. Guests expect you to be plump."

I winced.

Adele pressed the Pause button on the machine as her face fell and her eyes began to well with tears. "But you said—"

"I gave you three weeks, Adele. Four, if you count

what Andy told you the first day. You are now three sizes larger than Simone. Do you know what they're calling you around the palace? *Cinderblock!*"

I gasped, and so did the princesses. Valerie mumbled something in French that sounded like *le witch* while Miranda said to Laura, "That's not right." Laura made a fist and pounded it into the palm of her other hand. Tough one, that Snow White.

Adele said nothing. She kept her gaze straight ahead, focused on the poster that showed you how to take your pulse. She was like a zombie. Standing, breathing, but not there.

"Do you understand?" the Queen demanded.

"Yes," she answered robotically.

"Good. Then go upstairs, get your tiara, and turn it into Wardrobe. I've got just a few hours to suit Zoe up and train her to fill in for you."

Adele swiveled her head in my direction, her bland eyes targeting mine with the kind of fierce hostility you find in rabid dogs or angry drivers on the Turnpike. Her resentment was so palpable, I could feel it on my skin, burning hot.

"It's only temporary," I squeaked.

She tossed me the phone. "I bet you've been jacking up my weight on your stupid chart." She stepped off the cross trainer and put her icky, sweaty nose against mine.

"You planned this, so you could take my place as Cinderella."

"No! I've been knocking off ounces whenever I can."

"Then you admit you've been tampering with my chart. I knew it." She squirted water into her mouth and spit a stream into the wastebasket better than any jock I'd ever met. "I've had it with this place. I never wanted to play a princess, anyway. That's what my parents wanted, why they mortgaged the farm to send me to Fairyland camp year after year. I only tried so hard because I thought I could get a break here with my music, so screw all of you!"

We watched as Adele went into the girls' locker room and emerged with her pink Adidas bag over her shoulder, a white towel around her neck. Chin lifted high, she calmly left the gym, her sneakers padding softly down the hall.

Sixteen

Andy met me in Wardrobe, pacing anxiously while Trish did what she could to transform me, 5'10" Zoe Kiefer, into a delicate princess, practically sewing me into Adele's blue-and-white gown and stuffing my size-ten feet into clear plastic slippers. Once that ordeal was over, Helga the cosmetologist plunked me into a chair, yanked my hair into a super-tight ponytail, and proceeded to tweeze my eyebrows into tiny lines that, illogically, she then darkened with pencil.

"Stay still. Don't talk," she ordered.

Which was hard, because Andy was grilling me about the basics of Princess 101. Did I know how to wave? Did I know how to smile like a princess, to clasp my hands just so, as if I were a child who'd been surprised with a stack of birthday presents? Had I ever waltzed? Done the box step?

"I have one hour to teach you what took years of summer camp to teach Adele. You'd better be up to the task." Andy stroked his chin nervously as Helga pressed color into my lips. "She doesn't even come close to Simone."

"I'm doing what I can," she grumbled, applying blush with a big brush. "It's not like you've given me much to work with here."

Thanks. Thanks a lot for the vote of confidence, people. "Yeah, I think I know how to wave."

Helga pinched my mouth shut. "No talking! Close your eyes."

I closed my eyes.

Andy continued. "There's the dance with Prince Charming. It's more complicated than it looks."

I tried to recall what the dance was like. Lots of turning and waving, bowing and curtsying. Square-dancing with two royal squares.

"Open," Helga barked. I opened my eyes to the sight of her wielding what appeared to be a living centipede pinched between her fingers.

I let out a scream. "What *is* that?"

"Eyelashes. Now look up." I looked up as she pasted the sticky lashes to my lids. "Look down." I looked down.

Just when I thought this process couldn't get any more uncomfortable, they produced a heavy yellow-blond wig and two humongous fake diamond earrings that pulled down my earlobes like boulders. I slid off the chair, teetering under the weight of multiple petticoats. Trish stuffed my hands into tight white gloves. Helga fixed my lip gloss. At last, all three of my tormentors stepped back for the assessment.

"Walk!" Andy commanded.

So I walked.

He slapped his forehead. "No, no, no. Not like you're a construction worker just off from the job. Daintily, like a princess. Show some of that Wow! spirit."

My toes were killing me. I went up on them slightly, grimaced in pain, and pranced, Wow!™-like.

"That's better. Now twirl." He rotated his wrist. I twirled. I twirled so fast that, as I had in the Queen's office, I fell against the chair, and Trish had to come to my rescue.

"Enough, Andy," she said. "Take her into training."

Training was one big room with lots of mirrors and, playing on an eternal loop, the Fairyland theme song, to which I was taught the so-called Fairyland Family Dance. (Think the Hokey Pokey only with more twirling and kissing.)

Hands up! Twirl to the left, twirl to the left. Kiss! Kiss!

(Bottoms out!) Wave. Wave. Hands up! Twirl to the right, twirl to the right. Andy bow. Zoe curtsy. Air kiss. Air kiss. (Bottoms out!) Wave. Wave. Twirl to the left . . . and so on.

Practice over, Andy sufficiently exasperated, there was only one more detail that needed to be addressed: my tiara. Adele was supposed to drop it off, but she was nowhere to be found, and we were ready to go. Already the morning crew was returning from the park hot, sweaty, and tired in a well-coordinated choreography through secret doors. I was to switch with Simone at the top of Cinderella's staircase at four sharp. I couldn't do that, though, without my crown.

Dash passed me in the hall wearing his navy Prince Charming uniform. He stopped to give me a hug. "I took care of everything, Zoe. You're in the clear," he whispered. Then he jogged to catch up with the other princes.

That could have only meant that he'd snagged the Hansel's report about me. Unless Dash just wanted to give me a hug, which would have been fine, too. You know, I'm not one to complain.

I headed down the hall and found Jess and RJ chatting by the water fountain. He had one hand on the wall and was leaning into her while Jess was twirling her Red Riding Hood blond braid and playing coquette. I guess her night with Marcus had worked its magic, because, so

far, I'd never seen RJ so interested in another person . . .
besides himself.

"Hey," I said, hoping to grab Jess for a minute so I
could explain why I was Cinderella.

Jess took one look at me all dressed up and opened her
mouth in shock. "What's this about?"

"Long story," I said. "I'll go into it later. In the meantime don't believe any of the rumors. They're all lies." I
tried communicating on our nonverbal level by the usual
lifting of the eyebrows, rolling of the eyeballs, etcetera,
but Jess only said, "It's okay. I'm happy for you. You look
really good, Zoe."

No kidding. She was about to cry.

I took her aside. "Listen, you blond bubblehead of a
cousin, this is only temporary. Adele got demoted today,
and the Queen is making me fill in until she picks a permanent replacement. You should totally apply because . . ."

Adele was sauntering down the hall, tiara in hand.
"Hey, Jess. Look what your roommate got for ratting out
you and Marcus to the Queen."

Jess turned to me, aghast. "You *told* her?"

"No. Of course, not."

"Then quit running your mouth, Adele." Jess made
the most of her five-feet-four inches, stepping between
me and my accuser. "You don't know what you're talking
about."

"Uh-huh. Keep telling yourself that, little Jess. Trust me, your cousin is a backstabber who doesn't give a damn about you." Adele pushed herself between us and stuck the tiara into my wig. "Here. You finally got what you wanted."

RJ the senior statesman tried to take control. "Listen, people, this happens every summer. The Queen does a staff reshuffling, and egos get bruised, and suddenly the accusations start flying. Why don't we all take a deep . . ."

"Screw you, hipster!" Adele barked. "I'm so sick of you always telling us what to do. You're nothing but a freaking babysitter."

Jess gasped and patted RJ's arm. "That's not true," she gushed, as if any of us really thought he was.

Karl, his face red and sweaty, was coming down the hall in his wolf costume, carrying his smelly head. He took one look at the fracas and spun right around, heading in the opposite direction.

"RJ does have a point," I said, attempting to appeal to Adele's questionable sense of reason. "This is just an Ordinary Cast—"

Adele slapped her hand over my mouth. "Shut up and listen. You'll be Cinderella, and you'll get the twenty-five thousand dollars that should be mine. But this is not the end, Kiefer. You're going to pay for messing with me."

Enough! I'd had it with this high school melodrama.

Reaching into the pocket of my dress, I found the Queen's letter to Adele that she'd requested I deliver earlier and stuffed it down the front of her hot-pink spandex tank. "Here, liar. You'd better read this before you go making a fool of yourself."

The first buzzer rang. Our cue to get in place.

RJ slipped his arm around my waist. "Come on, Zoe. I'll show you where to go. Let's get away from the crazy girl."

We got to the top of the stairs, where Simone was waiting impatiently. "Wait. What's she doing here? Where's Adele?"

RJ said, "Just go, Zoe. I'll fill in Simone."

I descended the stairs and walked onto the stage, where a huge crowd of eager faces awaited. Toddlers sat on their fathers' shoulders. Mothers held cameras poised to click and shoot. These good people trusted us to put on a terrific show, one worth the steep admission fee and the long, hot drive down the Garden State, and I was about to ruin their expensive trip with one disastrous performance.

"Wave!" Valerie in her rose-colored Sleeping Beauty gown was waving madly, first with her right arm, then her left.

I waved.

"Twirl!" ordered Laura, dressed as Snow White with

her big, puffy red-and-white-striped sleeves. "Hold out your petticoat. Don't forget to curtsy! That's what Cinderella does."

Could the crowd hear them? I hoped not as I tried to coordinate waving with twirling and holding out my petticoat. Valerie and Laura were just standing there waving and blowing kisses while I was like some messed-up toy monkey on meth, twirling and waving and dipping crazily off to the side. I was so dizzy that, once, my foot slipped and I nearly pitched into a couple of kids.

Ian rode up on his horse and, at the sight of me bobbing about, quickly dismounted, handed the reins to a troll, and took the steps of the palace two at a time, grabbing me in what the audience interpreted as a Prince Charming clutch of passion but what was obviously his practical effort to gain some control.

"What are you doing?" he hissed.

I blinked, trying to stop the world from spinning. "Twirling and waving. That's what they told me to do."

He shot a reproving glance at Valerie and Laura, who were giggling behind white gloves. "Don't listen to them. They're just sticking up for Adele."

Well, it was nice that they were supportive. I'd heard so much gossip about the princesses being catty.

Ian lifted his right hand. I slapped it hard.

"No, no, no. You're supposed to take it," he said. "This

is the waltz. Not a basketball game."

Now a few parents were laughing as the crowd grew restless. Ian gripped my hand and circled my waist with his arm. "Not too close," he said. "This dance is rated G."

"As in 'gee I hate you'?" I gave him a dirty look.

He shook his head. "You've got it all wrong. Just dance."

The music started—*The Blue Danube* or something equally waltzlike—and next I knew it was back to twirling. I tried to pull him one way, but he only pulled me the other.

"You're leading," he said, like that was a bad thing. "Relax and follow me."

I wanted to tell him that no way would I ever follow him. "You used what I told you last night on the way to the party to invent a story about seeing Marcus in the Forbidden Zone. I would never let you lead me anywhere."

"Can we talk about this later?" he murmured into my ear. "Now is not the time or place for a fight. Okay, here's the float."

The giant royal float had arrived to begin the parade around the park. Rapunzel and her prince stepped onto it from the stage, then Snow White and her prince, and Sleeping Beauty with Dash.

Ian and I were the main attraction, our hands held artificially high as we took our places front and center. I'd briefly managed to catch sight of the Queen sitting on her throne behind us and noticed she appeared a touch green.

Perhaps she had ingested a rancid almond for lunch.

The float started up and, thanks to quick thinking on Ian's part, I did not fall off as it lurched forward. He took my hands and planted an air kiss near my lips. "Try to look enthusiastic. We are supposed to be enchanting, you know, not homicidal."

Easy for him to say. The music switched to the Fairyland theme song—"We Are Family"—and wouldn't you know it, there was another dance. Only, we had to do it on a moving float. I was doomed.

Ian raised his hand again. This time I knew better than to slap it. "I remembered," I said, putting my white glove gently in his.

He shook it off. "Actually, Zoe, we're doing the dance Andy supposedly taught you in the training room."

Oh. *That* dance. Right. Ian bowed. I curtsied, and it was hands up again without touching. *Twirl to the left, twirl to the left. Kiss! Kiss! (Bottoms out.) Wave. Wave. Hands up! Twirl to the right, twirl to the right. Ian bow. Zoe curtsy. Kiss. Kiss. (Bottoms out!) Wave. Wave. Twirl to the left.*

Wait . . . what was Dash doing all the way over there on the opposite side of the float? And why was he laughing?

I looked to the Queen for a hint, but she had her face in her hands. Dash sashayed near me and said, "Just pretend you know what you're doing, and no one in the audience will be aware. Old theater trick."

It was too late. People were pointing and taking pictures. One father called out in a heavy Jersey accent, "You need more practice, sweetheart!" Another said, "That's a ditzy blond for ya!" I would have leaped off the float and socked him if the parade hadn't come full circle back to the Princess Palace.

The nightmare was over.

We all lined up on the steps of the palace, took our bows, and proceeded inside, the Queen taking up the rear as kids gleefully booed her exit.

Once we were in Our World, she made a beeline in my direction. "Needless to say, that was a disaster." She removed her black gloves finger by finger as if picking off my numerous mistakes. "We need to find a permanent replacement for you immediately if not sooner."

I did my best to seem disappointed in order to hide my deep, deep relief. I never, ever wanted to do that again. Ever. Taking back-to-back SATs on a sunny June morning while getting my teeth drilled without novocaine would have been better. "I'm sorry, ma'am. I guess I'm not cut out for princess work."

"*Hmph.* That's an understatement." She handed me

her gloves, which I inferred meant I was back to being her assistant.

"The good news," I said brightly, "is that I know someone who can step in as Cinderella without a hitch. My cousin Jess."

The Queen's icy gaze scanned the hall for signs of Jess, who was laughing with RJ and Ian—probably about my debut.

"Do you mean Red Riding Hood Number Two? I can't say she's ever struck me as princess material. Did she graduate from one of our camps?"

I shook my head. "But she's been preparing for the part on her own since she was six. I swear, you won't have to teach her so much as a dance step."

The Queen sighed. "Well, we're in a bind, so I'm afraid she'll have to do."

It was happening. Yes! I tried to suppress my smile. "You won't regret it."

"For your sake, I hope not. Tell her to be in my office by eight tomorrow morning for an audition, and for heaven's sake, get out of that costume. Never in my life have I seen such a pathetic Cinderella."

On that sour note, she left, her purple-and-black cape flying behind her. I wriggled through the crowd to tell Jess, who seemed to have disappeared, so I went to Wardrobe, ripping off my wig and false eyelashes and stepping out of the mega-hot gown. I was hoisting it onto a hanger when something fell out of a pocket: a green, sparkly Fairyland envelope addressed to Adele.

Uh-oh.

If this was the Queen's letter to Adele, then . . . what letter had I given her?

Dash poked his head inside the dressing room, completely ignoring Rule #71: *No boys in girls' dressing rooms and vice versa.* "I see you got it."

"Got what?" I asked as tiny flames of panic licked my nerves.

He pointed to the envelope. "The Hansel's report. I took it from the troll before he could get to the Queen. Made some excuse about it being mine."

I rewound the order of events. Dash hugging me on the way to switching places with Simone. Me shoving the letter in Adele's top after she made that snarky comment about my backstabbing. I hadn't bothered to check that it was the right letter. Then again I'd had no reason to think there might have been two, since I hadn't felt Dash slip the letter into my pocket, thanks to all these freaking petticoats.

Which meant Adele, who loathed me with a vengeance, now held the one piece of evidence that could get me kicked out of the internship, a detailed accounting of how I'd rendezvoused with the traitor in the Forbidden

Zone and been so close to him, we could have kissed.

But what neither Adele nor Jake the Hansel knew was not only had I met and protected the traitor, I'd also lied to the Queen and said that I hadn't.

Not exactly what you'd call a Wow!™ moment.

Seventeen

I stood outside Adele's door and craned my neck to see if anyone was coming. I was definitely not supposed to be in the Princess Tower after hours uninvited per Rule #89: *Ordinary Cast Members (OCMs) should not be in the Royal Towers without permission after 8:00 p.m.*

A troll out in the lobby was playing FreeCell and sneaking past her had been a piece of cake. No, really. A piece of devil's food cake with coconut filling that I'd pilfered from the cafeteria.

The other interns were in the rec room for the Sunday night meeting followed by the weekly sundae-and-a-movie, a Fairyland tradition that was supposed to boost cast morale. I really wanted to see the feature film *The*

Avengers again, but not as much as I wanted to wrest the Hansel's report from Adele—and since she hadn't been at the meeting, I figured she was in her room sulking.

But her room was strangely silent.

I knocked softly. "Open up. It's me, Zoe. I need to talk to you."

Still, nothing—and now I was getting worried. You never knew what harm people were capable of doing to themselves, especially a person whose farming family back in Wisconsin had scraped and saved to send her to Fairyland summer camp.

I knocked again as footsteps came up the hall. The troll thundered toward me, traces of chocolate at the corners of her lips. "Hey. You're not supposed to be here."

"I'm not?" I splayed my fingers on my chest innocently as I often do when I'm about to tell a whopper of a lie. "But I'm the new Cinderella. Adele's replacement." I held up my master key. "See? Look, I'll open and show you."

Sliding the key in the lock, I turned once, and the door sprung open. The troll flicked the switch to reveal an unnerving scene. Adele's bed was unmade, clothes thrown everywhere as if the drawers had been ransacked. Shards of glass sparkled under the overhead light. Seemed Adele had shattered her three mirrors into a bazillion tiny pieces. How had no one heard this?

There was no sign of Adele.

"What the . . . ?" The troll reached for her radio to call her fellow troll cohorts. "Yeah, we got a suspected ten-ten in room four-oh-three. Looks like an AWOL Cinderella with potential anger issues. Uh-huh. May be armed with glass and dangerous."

I rolled my eyes. The trolls loved nothing more than overreacting to a situation. "She's not *dangerous*."

The troll pressed her Mute button. "Who's the security person here? Why don't you go to Maintenance and see if there's another available room? This one we're gonna have to mark off as a crime scene."

Really? *A crime scene?* I took two steps down the hall and stopped. What if it *was* a crime scene, though? Maybe Adele was in serious trouble.

And all because of me.

The next morning I arrived a little worse for wear, carrying the Queen's usual tray of tiny food and edited newspapers to find the office empty except for none other than the two-faced, deceitful, conniving, hardly charming Prince Ian.

In all the confusion of twirling and dipping and quite generally making an ass out of myself the day before, I hadn't taken note of Wardrobe's changes. Ian's messy mop of black hair had been trimmed to royal perfection, and any traces of his five o'clock shadow had been removed to reveal a smooth jaw.

In his stiff white Prince Charming jacket—which buttoned up at the throat, complete with a dark blue sash, gold buttons, and epaulets—Ian came off as almost *regal*. That is, for a snake.

He smiled shyly, though I couldn't tell if he was ashamed of the uniform . . . or what he'd done to get it. "I know what you're going to say. . . ."

"That you're a lying jerk who uses people? Good. End of conversation." I went over to the stack of mail the trolls had dumped on the table and sorted through the letters, postcards, catalogs, and important stuff as if he weren't there. He may have gotten what he wanted from the Queen, but he would not get anything more from me.

"Does this mean congratulations aren't in order?" he asked, hopping off the Queen's desk, where he'd been sitting and leaning over my table.

"For weaseling yourself closer to winning the Dream and Do? Not likely."

"I didn't weasel my way into anything. I still can't understand what your problem is. What did I do wrong?"

"You know." Three offers for cruises run by the Mouse. I ripped them into pieces and dumped them in the recycling bin.

"Wait, I get it." He stood back and nodded. "You're bummed that *I'm* a Prince Charming. . . ."

"Getting warmer."

". . . when you're no longer a Cinderella. And I don't blame you. We could have made such a lovely pair." He clasped his hands and batted his eyelashes.

I gathered up the junk mail. "You know what amazes me? It's that a head as tiny and pointed as yours has enough room for your oversize ego."

"That's not the only thing of mine that's oversize." He winked. "Wait, that was inappropriate, right?"

"And moronic." I dropped everything into the recycling bin. "You really need to get a clue, Ian. You are dead to me. Forever."

"Don't be bitter, Zoe, just because you're no longer royalty and I am."

My fingers curled, ready to strangle him. "I'm not bitter, and I never wanted to be Cinderella. I was only filling in on an emergency."

"And you did an admirable job if I do say so myself." He trailed behind me to the mini fridge, where we kept the caviar for Tinker Bell. "I personally thought your interpretation of the legendary ballet *Der Spastics* was fantastic."

I forced myself not to smile as I spooned Tinker Bell's smoked fish eggs into her crystal bowl.

"To turn left when everyone else is turning right. To clap at random. To twirl alone." He sighed deeply. "Sure, some might call your interpretation, oh, I don't know, *whacked*. But I prefer to think of it as genius."

For that I gave him a punch, hard, in the shoulder. Staying mad at Ian Davidson was impossible and, in some ways, that made me resent him even more. You could tell he'd be the type to go through life charming everyone in his path, blissfully unaware of the havoc he wreaked.

The side door to the Queen's private chambers opened, and she bustled in carrying Tinker Bell, with Andy following behind. Her Majesty must have been in a good mood, because for once her complexion bore the faintest hint of color.

"Ian, you look amazing. Promenade!" She sipped her tea while Ian, bold as brass, took long, exaggerated strides, head back, hand on hip, like he was on the catwalk in Milan. I had to bite the insides of my cheek to keep from laughing.

"Tell me you're not going to go out there like that," she said, the slightest hint of a smile playing on her lips, too.

"Of course not. I'll be like this." He bowed deeply before me and slipped to one knee, taking my hand in his and gazing with the perfect Fairyland combination of princely adoration and chaste love. Andy actually applauded, and even my own heart skipped a beat—which Ian must have felt because he squeezed my fingers gently.

"Am I forgiven, dearest?" he asked again, batting his eyelashes.

I mouthed, *In your dreams!*

The Queen nodded her rare approval. "That will do, Romeo." She motioned for him to stand. "And the dance . . . ?"

At this point I had to interrupt. "Where's Jess?"

"Pardon?" The Queen pondered an almond.

"Jess Swynkowski. She was supposed to be here as Adele's replacement. We talked about her yesterday, remember?"

"Oh, that. Yes, well . . . there's been a change of plans."

My stomach lurched. No, this couldn't happen. Jess was all ready. We'd stayed up until dawn practicing everything, even dancing to "If You're a Princess and You Know It" while we walked Tink. In fact, I'd assumed she'd be here waiting and ready to audition when I got to work.

I couldn't stop myself. I had to say something. "You promised yesterday that you'd make Jess Cinderella."

The Queen nibbled the almond. "I did no such thing. I gave her permission to audition. Permission I have since withdrawn."

"But that's not fair. You didn't even give her a chance!"

Andy cleared his throat in admonition. "Excuse me, Zoe, but you're only an assistant here. You are not involved in personnel decisions."

"It's all right, Andrew. Zoe deserves to know, since

this involves her, too." The Queen retrieved a letter from her desk. At first I thought with horror that it was the Hansel's, but as she started reading, I realized it was from Adele.

Dear Management:

This is in response to your totally unfair punishment.

As you know, I've done everything possible to stay within the Fairyland guidelines and the contract I signed. However, thanks to your backstabbing assistant, one Zoe Kiefer, who was in charge of charting my weight, you think I gained more than I did. Now she's Cinderella just as she planned, and you've made me a Class B character.

I am hurt and offended.

So I'm out of here. But I'm not gone, okay? And Zoe knows why. Tell her that it's only a matter of time until I use the ammunition I have against her to get my revenge. Then you'll see that both you and I were wronged, that I didn't gain any weight, and that this is all Zoe's fault.

Yours faithfully,
Adele

I was shaken to my core.

A million thoughts ran through my mind: Adele definitely had the Hansel's complaint. She was going to use it against me. My life sucked. Adele hated me and was ungrateful, too. My life double-sucked with a cherry on top.

Ian squeezed my arm. I was so stunned, I didn't push him away.

"Nothing but rubbish," the Queen said, stuffing the letter back in the envelope. "Adele is one of those recalcitrant types who never should have been allowed in the program." She looked pointedly at Andy, as if Adele's acceptance had been entirely his fault. "However, her absence means that we're short one Class B character, so Sydney will have to stay as the Fairy Godmother while Jessica will have to remain as Red Riding Hood, since I need two. Simone is willing to do double duty as Cinderella if she doesn't have to do the resort breakfasts and dinners, so that's that."

I raised my hand. "What about me?"

"As Cinderella?" The Queen let out something between a laugh and a snort. "Oh, my dear, I believe we've learned our lesson after yesterday's fiasco."

"No, I mean, I could work as your assistant *and* Red Riding Hood. Doing both would be no problem. Go through the mail in the morning, play Red Riding Hood the rest of the day. With Red Riding Hood's costume, no one would see my face, not really, so I could run errands for you in between."

The Queen said, "Why on earth would you take on such a Herculean task?"

She scrutinized me—as did Ian, who, too, seemed baffled by why I would take on two jobs for my cousin.

How to explain that Jess had been there during the slog of Mom's sickness when a lot of my other friends had fled? I couldn't. It wasn't just that I'd vowed none of the other interns at Fairyland would know me as the Girl Whose Mother Died, it was that Jess's quiet optimism, her reassurances that everything would be okay during those dark days, had saved me in ways no one else could understand.

"Because," I finally said, "Jess is going to blow your mind as Cinderella."

The Queen lifted one corner of her mouth, which could have been mistaken on a normal person for a sign of affection. Even weirder, she reminded me of my mother at that moment. "That's very Wow! of you, Zoe."

"Thank you," I said. "I think."

A second later Her Majesty was back to her old bossy self, and I was almost relieved when she started barking orders. "Gadzooks! We shall try it. Andy, message Wardrobe and tell them to get to work on Jessica. Meanwhile, if your morning chores are done, Zoe, proceed to Our World and suit up as Red Riding Hood. There's really nothing to it. 'My, Grandmother, what big . . .' and then name an essential body part. The juveniles adore it."

"Best of all," Andy said, "no dancing."

I gushed in gratitude, swore on everything I held dear that I wouldn't let her down, and clutched the folds of my gown to run as fast as I could to find Jess. I couldn't wait to hear her scream her head off.

"Hold up!" It was Ian running down the hall after me. "You forgot something."

I was already out of breath from my excitement. "I did?"

"Yeah, this. . . ." He reached out and put a hand on my shoulder. "You forgot to say good-bye."

Okay. "Good-bye."

He grinned in the goofiest way, like he knew something I didn't. Then he turned and went back to the Queen's office.

I would never understand Ian Davidson. Ever.

Eighteen

"You look perfect!" Jess straightened my wig with its long, blond pigtails and tied the red hood under my chin.

The outfit was ridiculous. A blue-and-white gingham dress, white ankle socks that did my legs no favors, shiny black shoes, and a huge red cape. I must have been the tallest Red Riding Hood ever, coming in just a hair under Karl the Wolf, who wasn't exactly a shrimp himself.

Jess, meanwhile, was gorgeous in her shimmering blue gown that perfectly matched her eyes. She didn't mind the gazillion petticoats or that the Cinderella wig and crown made it feel like you were balancing a set of tires on your head. It was as though she'd been born to live in huge black false eyelashes and white gloves and prance about in tiny shoes.

"I could wear this to sleep!" she exclaimed, spinning so hard, I could see her legs in her pale blue stockings.

Andy agreed that there was nothing left to teach. "She's a natural just as you described," he said, when we were watching Ian and Jess execute a flawless dance right down to the appropriately chaste air kisses. They aligned their lips with pristine precision that was so innocent, even RJ thought it was sweet.

"You are perfect," he said, looking Jess up and down admiringly.

Jess bit her lower lip. "How perfect?"

RJ laughed. "Fishing?"

"Maybe." She half smiled. "I'm waiting. . . ."

He bent down and whispered something that made her giggle. If she weren't my best friend, I would have barfed. "Whatever, Jess, you're a far better Cinderella than Adele," I said.

"What's up with Adele? Has anyone heard from her?" she asked, slipping her hand into RJ's.

So I guess it's official, I thought. RJ and Jess were officially a thing. I tried to act like their holding hands and being all over each other was normal. "I have no idea."

We got halfway down the hall, and RJ got even bolder, circling his arm around Jess and pulling her into him. "Adele's not going to do anything. By now she's probably halfway back to Wisconsin, and after a couple of days at home you'll be the furthest thing from her mind."

The first buzzer sounded, our cue to find our places. Valerie, the gorgeous Sleeping Beauty, floated up the hall in her pink gown, Dash beside her. He took one look at me in my cape and made a face. "Now you're Red Riding Hood?"

"Next I'll be Prince Charming," I said. "So watch out."

"That's what I've been doing," he said. "Watching out for you."

I took that to mean he had my back.

Valerie cleared her throat, none too happy with this little exchange of pleasantries. "And who is this?" she asked, nodding to Jess.

"Um, that's Jessica Swynkowski." *What, have you been living in a bubble?* "She's Adele's permanent replacement."

Jess gave Valerie a confident two thumbs-up, and I took some comfort in knowing that my cousin, though naturally shy, was secretly as tough as nails. She wouldn't fall for the other princesses' tricks, as I had. Jess had this Cinderella thing down, and when Ian took his place next to her, the audience obviously agreed, applauding magnificently after their debut performance.

Everybody was getting what they wanted, even Ian, who I had to begrudgingly admit was a much more capable Prince Charming than Marcus, even if he had lied to get the job. The way Ian boldly galloped to the stage and elegantly dismounted was almost thrilling, a far cry from Marcus's plodding entrance, clutching the reins with white knuckles, sweat pouring down his face.

Finally, I thought, I'd achieved what I set out to do the first day at Fairyland—make Jess a princess. And now she was a mere bleached-blond Cinderella hair away from winning the twenty-five-thousand-dollar grant that could change her life. All I had to do was keep serving the Queen with my usual diligence—while ensuring that she continued to think of Jess and me as completely upstanding, loyal Fairyland interns—and the grant would be in the bag.

The only obstacle standing in our way of guaranteed success was Jake the Hansel's letter. Adele still had it— she'd made that clear in her farewell note to the Queen. The question was: Would she send it, or was RJ right when he claimed that once she got back to Wisconsin, all grudges would be forgotten?

Let's just say I had my concerns.

"Don't get near him, Red! It's a trick!"

Viviana, an adorable six-year-old girl all in pink with plastic beads in her pigtails, clutched my cape and held me back as the Wolf beckoned with his paw.

"Come closer, my dear, the better to see you." Karl

could really lay it on thick, rubbing his paws maliciously as he approached in matronly white pumps. (Very few guys could pull off a wolf costume *and* a J. C. Penney wardrobe with as much élan as Karl did.)

The gathering crowd of children was riveted. They covered their tiny mouths in anticipation. They gripped their mothers' hands when Viviana and I backed ourselves into a corner between the faux medieval clock tower and the faux medieval cobbler's shop on the faux medieval cobblestones.

"My, Grandma, *wha*, *wha*, what a big nose you have," I stuttered.

"The better to smell you with, my dear." Karl was twelve terrifying inches away.

Viviana screamed. I screamed. Karl covered his ears, and I took advantage of his auditory agony to tiptoe away with Viviana just as Ian arrived on his horse to save the day.

He reined to a stop and smiled with beneficent interest. "Is there a problem, good maidens?"

Viviana furiously waved toward Karl. "That wolf is trying to eat Red Riding Hood."

Karl hooked his blue plastic purse in the crook of his arm, straightened his flannel nightgown, and stuck out a hip.

Ian squinted. "You mean that kindly old grandmother?"

"He's *not* a grandmother!" the children protested. "He's a wolf!"

"Let me see about this alleged wolf," Ian said, sliding off his saddle and adjusting his white jacket.

"Oh, no, Your Highness, I was just saying hello to my granddaughter." Karl's falsetto voice was delightfully absurd. "I'm not a wolf. Not me. Oh, no."

"Yes, he is!" the children cried.

Karl and Ian faced off with each other while I had second thoughts. If Ian had to save us, what kind of message were we sending to little girls like Viviana? Weren't Viviana and I perfectly competent to save ourselves without the help of male intervention?

"Come on, Viviana," I said, taking her hand again. "We can handle this." And we charged ahead, planting ourselves between Ian and Karl as I reached up and removed the wolf's lace nightcap, the one item that, in Fairyland, apparently distinguished carnivorous wild animals from brownie-baking grandmothers.

"You're not my grandmother," I declared. "The children are right. You're a wolf, and I'm going to ask this prince to arrest you for trying to kidnap me!"

Karl gasped and wobbled off in his heels. The children cheered. Red Riding Hood was saved . . . until the 4:00 p.m. show.

I knelt down and handed Viviana a rainbow lollipop

from my basket for being such a brave ally. She rewarded me with a hug and a furtive "I love you, Red," before skipping off with her mother.

I gave Ian a reluctant grin. "Good job."

"Not too bad yourself," he said.

The iPhone buzzed in the pocket of my cape. "In my office," she ordered. "*Stat!*"

I slid my phone to Off and stepped behind Jack's Beanstalk. After checking to make sure no one was looking, I yanked open the dark green door, took the staircase down to Our World, and then the elevator to her office, where I discovered Her Majesty hunched over her keyboard, googling.

"Sit," she commanded.

I took a seat and pushed back my hood. It was pleasantly cool in here with the air-conditioning. During heat waves a girl could miss a climate-controlled office.

"I suppose I don't have to tell you who Sage Adams is," she said, exiting out of a video.

"He was a runner-up on *American Idol*." I decided to refrain from adding that he was also the celebrity crush of Karolynne, the sixteen-year-old mother-to-be from *Teenage Pregnant Nightmare*. "And now he's a professional singer."

"Depending on how you define the word *professional*. Or, for that matter, *singer*." The Queen pressed a button, and pages began to spit out of her printer. "Be that as it may, it seems the famous Mr. Adams has a longing to revisit the days of yore by stopping by Fairyland for a tour of his favorite childhood haunt. Corporate would like us to seize the opportunity to make him our spokesperson."

That wasn't a bad idea, actually. Sage was almost eighteen, on the cusp of adulthood. Tweens loved him. Teenagers abhorred him. And middle-aged mothers thought he was exactly the kind of boy their daughters should be dating.

"That's sensible," I said. "Sage Adams is big among middle schoolers."

"I'm glad you have so decreed, because Mr. Adams and his manager, a one rather odious Michelle Michaels, will be here within the week, and you, my young and loyal assistant, will be their—albeit mute—escort."

She lifted the stack of newly printed pages and deposited them in front of me with a *thud*. "Some light reading for you."

I gaped at the stack, wondering what possible relation it had with Sage Adams. "Why me?"

She crossed her arms and scowled. "Because I'm like a dragon, Zoe—dangerous, incendiary, and decidedly ancient. Mr. Adams would no more relate to me than I would relate to his juvenile music. What's his hit song again? I was just looking at it on the You Tubes."

"YouTube," I corrected. "It's 'Come Away, My Love.' The live version. It drives girls wild, because it makes it sound like he's going to fall in love with them onstage."

"How incredibly naive and, yet, I must admire his marketing savvy. Hmm." She perched herself elegantly in the chair. "Sing it for me."

"Really?" I was a lousy singer.

"Yes," she said. "Really. I would like to be able to quote the lyrics, if possible, during negotiations."

I couldn't sing it because I couldn't carry a tune, but I could say it.

> *"This is my love song to you*
> *I don't know who.*
> *But when I look out into the crowd and see*
> *You being wowed. I'll know you're the one.*
> *So don't be surprised if I step off this stage*
>   *and reach out and say*
> *Come away with me . . . my love."*

The Queen lifted her eyes to the ceiling. "On behalf of all that is good and melodic, Ludwig van Beethoven, I apologize. Now, to the matters at hand." She tapped the papers. "What you have there is a comprehensive list of Mr. Adams's likes, dislikes, and deal breakers. It is your mission to read through the lists and ensure that everything he has requested is ready by his arrival, though we are lacking an ETA."

I checked the first demand: *no raw broccoli*. As if Fairyland even served fresh vegetables. The Xbox 360 and feather-free pillows seemed easy enough, but the fair-trade 80 percent dark chocolate and peanut butter made from nongenetically altered peanuts had me stumped. This was New Jersey. Everything here was genetically altered.

"The thing is, ma'am," I began, uncertain of how to turn down her offer to escort Sage. "I'm probably not the best person to be handling Mr. Adams and his manager. I don't mean to seem rude, but I'm just not a fan."

"Which is why you are ideal." She hand-fed a piece of mozzarella from her Insalata Caprese to Tink. "Somewhere on that list you'll see that Mr. Adams specifically requested an escort of a nonfawning nature. Also you two do have something in common." She arched her eyebrow. "A deep and abiding nostalgia for Storytown. He's curious to see its remains."

That threw me for a loop.

I was surprised that a big star like Sage cared about Fairyland's precursor, too. Maybe he wasn't so commercial and awful after all.

I said, "I thought Storytown was long gone."

"Not entirely, though according to our engineers it is sinking fast into the soft New Jersey sand." She sipped her tea. "You haven't seen it, Zoe, because in the interest of protecting public safety, it's been secured behind a wall, out of sight in the Forbidden Zone."

Sinking! The wall! The Forbidden Zone! That must have been where I got trapped in the quicksand and was saved by Dash.

"And you want me to take him there?"

Her teacup slipped out of her hand, falling to the saucer with a clatter. "Heaven forbid! Only if you wish to send me to an early grave!" She whipped out her white Chinese fan and started waving it to cool herself from the shock of my suggestion. "Were Mr. Adams to see how Storytown has been allowed to slip—quite literally—into decay, there is no doubt he would reject our offer of spokesmanship. Such a blight on our property is, shall we say, déclassé.

"Indeed, your goal will be to avoid all talk of Storytown while buoying his impression of Fairyland, so that Storytown becomes nothing more than a footnote in his future poorly crafted, overhyped, ghostwritten autobiography."

I sighed. There was no arguing with the Queen when she had made up her mind.

"Moreover, Mr. Adams will be here on business. To wit, he will not sign autographs or personally entertain the flirtations of various interns. Nor will you inform said interns that he will be, is now, or has been, on the premises. *Do. You. Understand?*"

I nodded.

"Speak!"

"Yes, ma'am."

She sat back, somewhat mollified. "You should know, Zoe, that there are only ten candidates remaining for the Dream and Do grant, and they include you and the sweet, hardworking cousin who you admirably support and who has the Wow! spirit in abundance. It would be a tragedy if a mishap during Mr. Adams's visit reduced that number to eight."

I swallowed hard, my throat as dry and scratchy as sandpaper. "Yes, ma'am." *No pressure there!*

Her computer dinged, and the Queen swiveled to check her email. "Oh, dear. This is not good. Not good at all."

"Is everything okay?" I asked. Now that I thought of it, she had been looking paler than usual—if such a thing were possible.

She absently played with the ruby-scarab brooch on her dress. "It's Adele, I'm afraid. We received information this morning that she didn't fly home to Wisconsin as Personnel had arranged. According to this alert from Security, a survey of our cameras shows she hasn't left the park."

She was still here—waiting to get me.

"Where do you think she is?" I asked, trying not to act too nervous, though I was frantic.

"Not far. Perhaps hiding out in someone's room or in the Forbidden Zone. Security, naturally, is fanning the area." The Queen checked her email again. "It is one of the most dreadful crises to afflict a fairy-tale theme park, a Cinderella gone rogue. There's no telling what kind of mayhem a scorned princess can wreak. No telling at all."

Nineteen

I would have gone hunting for Adele myself if the Sage Adams Project, along with catering to the Queen and Tinker Bell plus playing Red Riding Hood, hadn't kept me busy from dawn to midnight.

According to Sage's bossy manager, Michelle, I was to arrange for a hybrid town car that would transport them from the Philadelphia airport to Fairyland. The town car was to be stocked with spring water in high-density polyethylene bottles, organic veggie chips, nonalcohol-based hand sanitizer, Trident White gum (flavor: peppermint), an iPad with 4G capability, sound-isolating ultracompact headphones, and the complete series of *South Park* downloaded and ready for viewing.

Once at Fairyland Sage was to be provided with a black trench coat and a Philadelphia Phillies baseball cap, because apparently *that* wouldn't make him stand out in a theme park in August. When we were introduced, I was not to say anything but "hello" and escort him and Michelle to the attraction of his choice.

Most importantly Michelle stressed, *"Do not talk."*

The visit was to take approximately three hours, no longer. At the end I was to usher him into Our World and then through the hidden tunnels to the Fairyland Kingdom Resort, specifically to room 505, the corner penthouse suite, where the TV was to be on and turned to MTV. The curtains were to be closed to prevent paparazzi from intruding.

The sheets on his bed were to be organic cotton, and all bedding was to be washed thoroughly in two-hundred-degree water before his arrival. The carpet was to be steam cleaned with nontoxic detergents. There was to be no leather, feathers, or any other animal product in the room. The windows should be washed with white vinegar and water. The soap in his bathroom: grapefruit/mint. Organic, natch.

There must have been fifty reminders that this visit was to be secret, confidential, blah, blah, blah. And if I so much as whispered the name *Sage*, the skies would open, and all hellfire and damnation would rain down on Fairyland.

It took me two days of ordering online from the Queen's office and then making sure everything was delivered to room 505 instead of being lost somewhere in Fairyland's cluttered mailroom. I even stood on chairs and washed the huge plate-glass windows in Sage's penthouse suite—all eight of them!—with vinegar and water. That alone took close to four hours. I'd never be able to move my arm again.

"Congratulations, you did it!" exclaimed Sergei, the hotelier. I'd thought he was a complete snob when we first met and I'd had to explain that I, not he, would be handling the arrangements for a "Special VIP" the Queen had forbidden me from naming.

Now, having bonded over the search for the thirty peace lilies that Michelle demanded because they "filtered" the air, Sergei and I were old buddies. He ran a finger over the top of the TV cabinet and nodded his approval when it came up clean. "Is there anything else?"

"Not until the actual day."

"And that is . . . ?" You could tell he was annoyed by our "Special VIP's" refusal to pinpoint the date of his arrival, which was saying something, since Sergei had handled his share of spoiled guests.

"Anytime after today, apparently. Doesn't matter. We're ready."

He opened the door using his handkerchief to prevent germs from tainting the knob, also one of Michelle's requests. "Are you coming?"

"I think I'll do one last inspection. Thanks."

"Very well." And he left.

I listened for his footsteps in the hall and went over to the TV, turning the volume *wayyy* down low as I clicked to channel 831. It was 9:00 p.m. on a Monday, and if memory served, *Teenage Pregnant Nightmare* would be playing in back-to-back reruns.

Yes, yes, of course, this violated a bunch of Fairyland rules, mostly #23 and #64. But it'd been ages since I'd watched TV, and I was suffering withdrawal, so you could consider this almost a mental-health excuse.

Karolynne came on with her new boyfriend, who went by one letter—Z. Ugh. What a loser! I sat on the settee at the foot of the king-size bed and studied Z. Wifebeater. Skanky beard. A bunch of gold chains. Clearly he was in it for the fame of being on *TPN*. I mean, he wasn't even Karolynne's type. She went for guys who were short and stocky. Z was tall and wiry and covered with weird red welts.

I was prepared to be riveted as Karolynne and Karolynne's slack-jawed sister, Tanya, cracked their gum while shopping for cribs—an episode I had found amusing in my wood-paneled TV room back in Bridgewater, but that now, after a summer of serving the Queen's wild whims, I found to be simply boring. Didn't these people have anything better to do? Like maybe get their GEDs?

Twenty minutes later and Karolynne was fighting with Z over why he hadn't gone shopping for cribs. (I swear she and Hunter Boxworth once had the exact same argument.) Their faces turned red. Z threw a lamp and yelled that he wasn't her baby's father. For that Karolynne's mother, Mae, doused him in her white wine. Even Karolynne tossed a pillow now and then. All this yelling and atrocious grammar and general nastiness gave me such a headache that I had to turn it off.

The Queen would have been appalled and rightly so. What had I ever seen in that show?

I closed the TV cabinet doors feeling somewhat blue. Without *TPN* to look forward to when I got home, there was nothing. Just me and Dad and school.

Well, I wouldn't think of leaving Fairyland now. I would think about that later. The old Scarlett O'Hara approach.

Gathering my Sage file, I stepped out of his suite to find none other than Dash Merrill waiting for the elevator in his Prince Charming getup.

"Dash?"

He did a double take. "Zoe?"

"What are you doing here?"

"Tuck-in service." He rubbed his fingers together to show it paid well.

Rich folks could afford to do this: arrange for a prince or princess to stop by their suites with milk and cookies to read bedtime stories to their children. While it wasn't exactly encouraged, parents often tipped heavily.

"How about you?" he asked, punching the button for the elevator again.

"Running an errand for the Queen." Vague enough.

The elevator dinged, and the doors opened. Dash waved me in. "After you."

As soon as the doors closed, he pressed the Stop button and folded his arms. "We have to talk."

"This with the stopping the elevators again. Your only move?"

"I tend to stick with what I know. Okay, what are we going to do about Marcus? I feel bad."

So did I. It was beyond unfair that he'd been kicked out for being the victim of mistaken identity. "Look at it this way: He's back in California and happily surfing again and, as far as Prince Charming goes, Ian's a huge hit. All's well that ends well, right?"

He shook his head. "I have to tell Her Majesty the truth."

A knot in my stomach tightened. "You do that, and you're out of the running for the Dream and Do grant."

"I know."

"There are only ten people left as it is."

"Really?" He sighed heavily. "And if we're not out already, we will be."

I suspected this was what he was getting at. "You're bringing me down with you?"

"I'm not bringing you down, Zoe. You're a witness. You were in the FZ that night. You know it wasn't Marcus you ran into, so you have a responsibility to come forward, too."

"I'm not *wholly* responsible," I said, repeating one of his better puns.

He didn't laugh, didn't even crack a smile. "What about the shirt swatch you found? Do you still have it?"

"I'm surprised you know about that."

"It was my shirt that got ripped, after all. If you show that to the Queen, it'll clear Marcus, who probably doesn't even own black flannel, seeing as how he's from Southern California. That's evidence right there that he's innocent."

The speaker came on. Hotel security telling us their computers indicated a stoppage between floors five and four.

Dash said, "Sorry. We'll get it back online." He pressed Resume. The elevator started up, and we descended, my brain reeling. Dash was right. I needed to step up and do the right thing, and I would . . . if it weren't for Jess.

"But what about the other night I saw you?" I asked.

"If I go to the Queen, she'll want to know what Marcus was doing then, and I'll have to say he was with my cousin, which will automatically disqualify her from the Dream and Do grant, too."

"Then there'll be seven candidates left." He shrugged. "C'est la vie. At least our consciences will be clear."

We got to the ground. Dash and I stepped out into a stark white, empty hallway by the service area. He was looking at me expectantly, waiting for my verdict.

"I don't get it," I said. "You were all gung ho to steal the Hansel's complaint so we wouldn't get caught. Now, all of a sudden, you're Mr. Honesty, and you're coming clean to the Queen. What happened?"

He grinned dopily. "Valerie. She and I are, um, pretty close these days, and I've told her everything. . . ."

I set my jaw, irked that he seemed to have forgotten his pass at me in the elevator. Was that really just a ruse to throw off the trolls? It certainly didn't feel like one, going by those kisses.

". . . and she convinced me that this is the right thing to do. How could I ever live with myself if I won the grant knowing that Marcus got screwed?"

"That's a *whole* other issue, Dash. Remember?"
But he didn't.
And that's how I knew. I was being set up.

Twenty

An hour later, Tinker Bell put to bed, I had showered out the hair spray from the day and was stepping into a clean pair of shorts when there was a knock on my door. Jess, still in her Cinderella makeup.

"We never see each other anymore, so when I saw your light was on, I thought I'd stop by." She flounced in and collapsed on her old bed, her new bed being in the sweet Princess Tower. "I miss you. I even miss this tiny, hot box."

When Jess was promoted to Cinderella, she'd timidly requested to stay as my roomie, and the Queen had ripped her a new one for having the audacity to reject the Princess Tower. Probably no one had ever asked the question, since—aside from a better chance of winning the Dream & Do—spacious, air-conditioned rooms were the major reason why cast members wanted to become royalty.

"You're better off where you are," I said. "It's quieter, so you can get more sleep."

"Sleep? What's that? Between working the breakfast and tuck-in shifts at the resort *plus* my regular shift in the park *plus* finding time to be with RJ, I've forgotten the concept."

I stuffed Ian's penlight into my pocket. "So you and RJ are still going strong, huh?"

She raised herself up on her elbows. "He's so sweet, Zoe, and he's really into me. Do you know he brings me coffee to my room every morning? And I have to get up at six!"

"Good. You deserve it." Though I wondered what would happen when the internship was over and Jess went back to high school and RJ to college. Those college/high school romances never seemed to work out.

Jess jerked her chin at the flashlight in my pocket. "Are you going out? Don't tell me the Queen's sending you on another one of her bogus late-night errands."

"This is for me." *For you.*

I told her about my "accidental" run-in with Dash that, on second thought, didn't seem so accidental after all. He'd been waiting for me. Jess listened, brows furrowed, but even she didn't understand until I spelled it out.

"He didn't get any of my hole puns. Therefore, Dash is not the prince."

She laughed. "So? He knew about the shirt, Zoe, and you, the prince, and I are the only ones who know about that. How much more proof do you need?"

I sighed in exasperation. "You had to be there in the woods those two nights, Jess. If Dash had been the real . . ."

Jess put her finger to her lips.

I crawled next to her on the bed and lowered my voice to a whisper. "If Dash had been the real prince in the woods, he would have at least acknowledged the puns in some way. I'm telling you, there wasn't even a flicker of recognition when I said '*wholly* responsible.' It meant nothing to him."

Jess lay back down again, arms crossed behind her head, thinking. "I've known you since the day you were born, Zoe. That's seventeen years and counting, and you're one of the most perceptive people I know. If your gut tells you that Dash is pushing you to confess to the Queen so he can whittle down the pool of candidates for the Dream and Do, then you're probably right."

Finally!

"Thank you." I got up and grabbed my sneakers. No flip-flops.

"You're going out there to find him, aren't you?" she asked.

"Someone has to," I said, yanking on my laces. "If Dash is going this far to get me disqualified, then we're all in trouble, including the so-called traitor. Dash wants to win the Dream and Do bad, if not for himself, then to please his father, and the only way to save ourselves is by getting to the truth."

"And if you find the real prince?"

I zipped up my school hoodie. "I have no idea. Kind of just planning on crossing that drawbridge when I get to it."

The clock tower struck eleven when I headed toward the forest an hour past curfew without Tinker Bell as an excuse. Two rules violated with a single step.

To me the park was most magical after the guests have left, and this night was no exception. The Little Mermaid's Falls shimmered with pink, blue, and yellow incandescence, and infinitesimal fairy lights twinkled in the trees. Here, the world was every inch a real fairyland.

A passing troll stopped to shine her flashlight in my direction, but then, recognizing me as the Queen's lady-in-waiting, gave me a begrudging nod and trudged onward. The trolls had been treating me with a certain deference lately. I could only conclude this meant my boss must have told them to give me carte blanche to do as I pleased so I could perform the necessary preparations for our Special VIP. Believe you me, the trolls weren't happy about this new agreement. They lived to bust us interns.

I'd just passed Snow White's Cottage when I heard voices up ahead that sounded like Dash and Valerie. Since they were the last people I wanted to see, I hid behind one of the fake trees used by the witches to terrorize children and made myself small. They strolled by, arms around each other, murmuring and kissing. I could have probably been lying dead on the ground and they would have stepped over my body and kept kissing, that's how absorbed they were in each other.

I waited for them to disappear over the hill to the Pied Piper's Glen before hopping back on the path. The park became darker and darker the farther I got into the Haunted Forest. As a cost-saving measure, the gaslights had been turned lower to a dull yellow.

Snap. A branch behind me broke as if it had been stepped on. I froze to get a read on the situation.

Another *snap.* Then the soft tread of footsteps.

I was being followed. *Yes!*

My heart kick-started into a fast beat along with a bracing shot of adrenaline. This wasn't a troll. Trolls tromped. It could have been another cast member out for a late-night walk—though, seeing as how I'd passed the fence to the Forbidden Zone, few would dare. The tiny rotating camera perched on top blinked its menacing red light. I stuck out my tongue at it when it swiveled in the opposite direction.

What I needed now was a lookout.

Latching on to an overhanging branch, I swung around silently and perched like a panther waiting to pounce. Meanwhile the footsteps got closer and closer, and my pulse pounded against my eardrums as I assessed the situation. From the stealthy way my follower also avoided the camera, by ducking down out of its range, I knew I'd found my prince.

He stopped a few feet away, sensing something. A stiff gust of wind blew, and I held on to my tree branch for dear life, praying my attacker wouldn't become curious and . . .

"Zoe? Is that you?"

There was another gust of wind, and I jumped. Or maybe I fell. Anyway, I landed on him with a heavy grunt.

"Oof!"

He buckled under my weight, his body crashing into the soft forest ground. I rolled him over, pinning his arms and straddling his back. Then I turned on Ian's penlight for a clear view of my would-be assailant.

"Hey!" he shouted. "I've been looking for that!"

No freaking way! I brushed aside his black hair. "Ian?"

With one swift move, his leg twisted around mine, and suddenly I was the one on the ground, and he was the one straddling me. "Never mess with a Texan. Haven't you seen the bumper stickers?"

"I thought it was 'Don't Mess with Texas.'"

"Literary license." He clucked his tongue in disappointment. "Man, I was so hoping the rumors Marcus spread before he left weren't true."

I spit out some pine needles. "What rumors?"

"That you're the Queen's snitch. You told on him and Jess, and now you're hiding out in the forest waiting to catch people for violating curfew to rack up more points." He rolled off and sat beside me, shrugging off his backpack. "And to think I've been sticking up for you."

"Don't even start. If anyone's a snitch around here, it's you," I said, wiping dirt off my chin.

"Yeah, right." He pulled a water bottle from the pocket of his backpack and unscrewed the top. "Because I'm the one hanging in trees like the monkey hall patrol." He offered me a sip.

I was too angry and insulted to accept. "Let's review the facts. *You* were the one lurking around the woods the other night when you saw me talking to the so-called traitor, and you scurried back to the Queen to tell her, so she could make you a Prince Charming. Now, you waited until I went into the woods so you could follow me for more incriminating evidence. It's so obvious."

"What the hell are you talking about?" He took another, bigger swig. "I had no idea you were out here."

"Then what are you doing in the Forbidden Zone past curfew?"

"It's past curfew?" He shrugged. "I never pay attention to that kind of thing."

"You're avoiding the question."

"No, I'm avoiding the answer. But, since you were the one who jumped me, I think it's only fair that you tell me why and what you were doing hanging in a tree."

Might as well. He was only going to blab to the Queen that he caught me in the FZ anyway. "If you wanna know the truth, I was trying to catch the traitor."

Ian flicked his finger at me. "Called it!"

"But not for the reasons you assume. Marcus got sent back to California, thanks to you, and now there are only ten people left who are eligible for the Dream and Do. Dash wants to reduce it to two—him and Valerie. Tonight he almost got me to confess to the Queen that I'd met the traitor twice in the FZ—"

"You can't do that," Ian said. "You promised."

I was about to tell him not to interrupt when I got confused. "Pardon?"

"The first night, when I pulled you from the quicksand, you said something about your being in my debt—though it seems to me since then you kind of forgot about all the nice stuff I'd done for you, such as saving your life. When we ran into each other next, you were all about being loyal to Fairyland."

I was speechless, unable to move my lips, which hung open in shock. I braced myself for the Ian-esque punch on the shoulder, for him to admit that he'd overheard this in the gym or that he'd listened in on my conversations with Jess. Because he hadn't even been a prince that first night. He'd been Puss 'n Boots. So he couldn't have had access to the cologne.

"Seriously, you can't go to the Queen. Just leave things as they are."

We sat in silence for a while as I tried to piece this together. "In other words, what you're saying is, as the witness instead of the perpetrator, I'm not wholly responsible."

"Nah. You don't want a stupid mistake like this to *hole-d* you down."

I winced. And smiled. "So you're the guy I've been running into?"

"Like I told you before, guilty as charged."

Then I remembered Marcus, and things didn't seem so rosy. "But that means you lied, Ian. You blamed Marcus for being the traitor slipping in and out of the FZ, when all along it had been you."

He wiped his mouth on his sleeve. "No, I didn't. Wow, you really do think I'm scum, don't you?"

"If the shoe fits . . ."

"As it always does in Fairyland. Then you should know I did tell the Queen. The day after the party at the Frog Prince's, after you said I was the prime suspect, I went to her office bright and early and came clean about why I'd been hiking at night and where I'd been going. I even told you that."

"I thought—"

"You thought I told her lies about Marcus. I know, I know. You've only said it a million times. But I never mentioned Marcus once."

"And yet you got his role as Prince Charming."

"Crazy, isn't it? She said I deserved it after working overtime teaching Marcus how to ride, for all that was worth, and for beefing up Puss 'n Boots so he wasn't just a secondary character. Guess I must have showed a lot of Wow! spirit or whatever."

Like Jess, I thought. But I was still confused. You could have all the Wow!™ spirit in the world and still be kicked out of the program for going into the Forbidden Zone. "I can't believe she didn't at least read you the riot act."

He shrugged. "Nope. The only condition was I not tell anyone, so do me a favor and keep this to yourself."

I slapped a mosquito that had been going to town on my ankle. "The bugs here are murder. I'm getting eaten alive."

Ian fished into his pack and pulled out a small plastic bottle. Flicking it open, he squirted some of its contents on the palms of his hands, rubbed them together, and then ran them over my legs. The fumes of the princely cologne instantly fogged my brain. Or maybe it was the effect of Ian's hands.

"The cologne?" I murmured.

"I got hold of a bottle the first day when I heard it was the best insect repellent ever. Guess that's to be expected with something from the Amazon." He stood and picked up his backpack while I tried to process that Ian had been using the valuable essence of some rare South American orchid as basically Deep Woods Off!.

"Where are you going?" I asked as he headed away from Fairyland.

"To my usual campsite." He nodded westward. "The stars are spectacular out there. Wanna come?"

"Now?" Trespassing into the Forbidden Zone was bad enough. Spending the night was out of the question. "I can't. If the Queen found out, she'd . . ."

"Make you a princess like she did me a prince?" He chuckled. "Look, Zoe, we've only got a few more weeks here. We're not going to be sent home at this stage.

Besides, I'm not going to win the Dream and Do, and probably you're not either, and your coming with me won't be a black mark on Jess, which is what I know you worry about. So, why not?"

When he said this, it was like he had lifted a heavy burden from my shoulders, a weight I hadn't known I was carrying. Ian was right. *Why not?*

And so, I took his hand and followed him deeper into the woods simply because I had nothing to lose.

Twenty-one

We eventually emerged from the forest into a field where frogs croaked in harmony with a chorus of crickets. Even a few fireflies, stragglers from the early summer, rose from the grasses, twinkling to disappear among the stars. A waning moon shed an almost ethereal white light on the rubble of some ancient foundation.

Ian and I scaled the stones and arrived at the edge of a large, still pond reflecting the night sky. Rimmed by a sandy beach and protected by scrub pines, it was so pristine and untouched that I went, "Whoa!" a tad too loudly, causing the frogs to quit croaking and hop into the pond with a *plop, plop.*

"Nice, isn't it?" Ian asked, smiling in the moonlight.

"We don't have anything like this back in Bridgewater. Can you swim in it?" I'd heard lakes in the Pinelands were gross and swampy.

"Oh, yeah. It's fed by a spring, and the bottom as far as I can tell is almost all sand." He dropped his backpack onto the rocks, crossed his arms over his head, and pulled off his T-shirt. I tried not to look, but he was a Prince Charming, after all, and let's just say he met the minimum requirements.

Ian stood at the edge of the rubble, hands on hips. "It's a dammed-up stream left from when there used to be a gristmill here, so it's pretty shallow." He put his arms out and dove in like a racer, skimming the surface.

I hadn't brought a swimsuit, of course, so I sat on the rocks hugging my knees and feeling awkward.

Ian's head popped out in the middle of the pond. "Come on in!"

"I don't have a suit."

"So what? I don't care. Do you?"

Um, yeah. "I think I'll pass." Anyway, my toes were already curling at the prospect of frogs or fish below. I was a Jersey girl. We didn't do ponds and fresh water. We did cement and chlorine.

"Don't be a wimp, Kiefer. Come on in. I know you wanna."

That was true, too, though mostly because I didn't want Ian thinking I was such a prude that I was afraid to get my tank top wet. Without a passing thought as to whether this violated the Fairyland morality clause, I stepped out of my sneakers and shorts, shrugged off my shirt, and, wearing just my tank and underwear, ran off the rocks before I could chicken out.

Ian was right. The water felt wonderfully cool and smooth after the sticky-hot hike, and I was able to graze the sandy bottom before I surfaced, careful to keep my legs moving lest there be sea monsters.

"Isn't it awesome?" Ian swam next to me and shook off the water. I didn't know if he was going to be one of those guys who liked to torture girls by pulling them under and pushing them down, so I was relieved when he left me alone to float on his back and look at the stars.

"How'd you find this place?" I asked, doing the same. I'd never seen so many stars in my life. It had to be because there wasn't any ambient light from a city or the interstate.

"Saw it on a map before I got here and decided to check it out. That's the major reason why I agreed to do this internship, because of the Pinelands. Do you know there are actually carnivorous plants around here?"

My toes did that curling thing again. "In the water?"

"Not to my knowledge or information." He laughed. "My dad's a lawyer, and that's how he answers every question, no matter how small. 'Not to my knowledge or information.'"

I had the feeling Ian was a big fan of his dad and of Colorado, where they used to live and hike every weekend. As we floated around, he told me how his parents separated a few years before and he had to leave his beloved mountains for Dallas so his mother could take a new job. He hadn't exactly been thrilled by the relocation.

"Everything's so artificial in Dallas. We live in a gated community where the grass is chemical green, the pools are chemical blue. For fun, everyone goes to the mall or drives around in big air-conditioned cars, sits in air-conditioned theaters. I miss woods like this. I miss being able to walk out my door and be surrounded by nothing but wilderness."

It seemed like a funny observation from a guy who was interning at a totally artificial fairy-tale theme park.

Our feet touched, and Ian ran his foot along my ankle. I didn't pull away.

"I'd had a job lined up at an outdoor gear store in Telluride, but . . . my dad's new wife didn't think that would work."

Ouch! My heart twinged in sympathy. "And Dallas?"

"If I'd stayed in Dallas, Mom would have made me work all summer."

"Work never killed anyone, as my dad likes to say."

Ian paused. "As a model."

Oh.

Actually this didn't come as that big of a shock. I'd heard rumors that some of the cast members had worked as models, Ian included.

"So you really are a Hollister dude, huh?" I asked.

"It's mega embarrassing. My mother got me into it after the divorce because she said we were broke and I needed the money for college. Between you and me, I think she loves the whole scene, the agents, the photographers, the cash. She'd have me quit school and do it full-time if she could get away with it."

"And if you didn't want to be a naturalist . . ."

He stopped floating and looked at me. "How very perceptive of you, Kiefer. As a matter of fact, that is kind of what I'm interested in, and I've been thinking a lot about Yale's forestry school." He went back to swimming. "How about you? What do you want to do?"

I lay in the water staring up at the stars thinking how, unlike Fairyland, they had been here long before I was born and would be here long after. That filled me with a comforting peace, as if the universe had just given me permission to simply enjoy being alive here in the pond with Ian under the vast night sky, instead of constantly worrying about the Dream & Do grant and Jess and whether I was in trouble.

I said, "I don't ever want to leave."

"That," he agreed, "is an excellent idea."

* * *

After we got out of the water and I wrapped myself in Ian's towel, we sat on the rocks and ate apples Ian had brought and chatted about Fairyland and what it was like to work for the Queen and who was most likely to win the twenty-five thousand dollars. (We always came back to Dash and Valerie.) When I felt my tank top was as dry as it was going to get, I got back into my shorts and threw on my shirt.

Except I'd grabbed Ian's by accident.

"This is the one you ripped on the thorns," I said, fingering the flannel. "Dash said it was his."

"He did, did he? How clever of him." Ian took a last bite of his apple, stood, and chucked the core into the weeds. "Was this part of his plan to get you to confess to the Queen that you'd been in the FZ?"

"Yep. To be fair to Dash"—and it was not easy being fair to Dash—"it sounds like his parents are really pressuring him to bring home the grant. He told me that when his dad dropped him off at the airport, he mentioned all the money they'd spent on Fairyland camps that could have sent the family to Europe. Talk about guilt."

Ian sat back down next to me so our thighs were touching. "If I'd ever said to Dad that I wanted to go to a Fairyland camp, he would have signed me up for the marines."

I laughed. "I never thought of it that way, but you're

right. My dad has no clue, either."

"It's the mothers you've gotta watch out for. They're the ones behind the scenes micromanaging every detail, making you think something they want you to do is really your idea."

I kept silent as I always do when people start griping about their mothers.

Ian must have sensed that he'd overstepped some sort of boundary, because he added, "But I'm sure your mother's nothing like that, right?"

"Uh-huh."

More silence. I hugged my knees tightly. After a few minutes of this painful awkwardness, Ian asked softly, "Did I just say something wrong? I do that, you know. A. Lot."

Oh, god. Exactly what I wanted to avoid. If I said, "I don't want to talk about it," I'd come off as rude. And yet, if I did relay the morose story about losing Mom, Ian would probably pull a move like my funeral-boyfriend, Derek James, and get as far and as fast away from me as possible.

This was the one vow Jess and I had made to each other: No one would know about her family's "downturn in finances," as the Swynkowskis put it, and no one would know about Mom. But if there was one lesson I'd learned during this summer, it was that some rules are worthwhile, and others need to be broken.

I said bluntly, "My mom's gone."

"Oh." He pushed a stone with his foot. "I was afraid it was something like that. When did she leave?"

"She didn't leave. I mean, not willingly." I took a big, cleansing breath like Ari, my grief counselor, said I should in these situations. "She died. A year and a half ago, after being sick forever."

Dammit! As I feared saying that out loud triggered the familiar dreaded reaction. My eyes suddenly burned. My nose tingled. I was going to cry, and there was nothing I could do to stop it.

"I miss her every day." My voice choked.

Ian said, "Come here." His arm slid around me, drawing me to him, and he gently pressed my head to his shoulder. We sat like that until my sobs subsided and I could be a normal human again.

"Sorry," I said. "I try not to do that."

"It's your mom. I totally get it."

We were silent again, so quiet that the frogs had enough confidence to start up. "I really like being here, Ian. With you."

He didn't say anything, and I was worried that I'd come across as too needy, what with the crying and then the sappy admission that I liked him. I started to wiggle away, but he only held me tighter.

"Would you think I was scum if I made a pass at you right now?" he asked.

I smiled to myself. "That depends. Do you want to kiss me because you just found out I'm a tragic figure? Or is this your thing, hitting on girls who've lost their mothers?"

"Zoe," he said, with complete and utter seriousness, "I'm not gonna lie. I've wanted to kiss you every day since I saw you at orientation making an ass out of yourself with Dash."

"It was Dash who—" But I didn't get a chance to finish. He thumbed a few remaining tears off my cheeks and hesitated.

"You okay with this?"

"With what?" My pulse had started pounding so hard, it had drowned out every sound except for my beating heart.

"I know you've been through a tough time, and I don't want to—"

Oh, please. I brought my hand to the back of his neck and pulled him down. At the touch of his lips on mine, I quivered, and—sensing this—he wrapped me in his arms to steady me.

We broke away, and he shook his head. "Wow. And I do not mean that in the Fairyland sense of the word."

"I know, right?" I laughed.

"Let's try that again just to make sure it was legit." This time I let him make the first move. And this time we didn't break away.

Somehow we got off the rocks and onto the beach, falling onto the sand, laughing. Next I knew he was on top of me, kissing me and stroking my hair and all I kept thinking was, *He's a Hollister model*. How rad is that?

I wanted him to keep going, but he rolled off and rested on one elbow, just looking at me and grinning.

I said, "What?"

"I was just remembering you that first day, how self-righteous you were about everything. You were like some sort of ice princess."

"I was so not an ice princess." Valerie. She was an ice princess.

"Really? You jumped all over me for asking you a simple question. I thought you were going to bite off my head when I dared to question why you're a vegan."

I ran a finger up his arm, wishing maybe we could stop talking and go back to what we were doing. "So I scared you is what you're saying."

"You had me kind of alarmed, yeah."

"Even with your posse of cannibalistic chickens?"

He leaned over and kissed me lightly. "Don't dis the chickens."

I kissed him back. "You know what? I just realized

that this is one of the most perfectly happy nights I've ever had."

"Not *the* happiest night you've ever had? I'm very goal-driven, so I need to know."

I lay back and thought about perfect happiness as I took in the stars, the warmth of the beach, the sound of the frogs croaking in the soft air, and gorgeous Ian Davidson lying next to me, so near I could feel the heat off his body. "Almost. Not quite perfectly happy, but close."

"Well, let's see if we can improve on that." And he kissed me again.

Twenty-two

I blinked and looked down at my hands entangled in another's. There were my fingers—I recognized the pink nail polish sparkling in the bright morning sun—but whose fingers were those?

Ian's!

Rolling from his grasp, I sat up in alarm. We'd spent the night together! Outside Fairyland! Those violations were so egregious, they weren't even in the handbook.

And then another crushing epiphany: *Tinker Bell.*

I could just picture her tiny white paw frantically pressing the brass buzzer for the Queen, the doggy version of tattling that I hadn't been there to walk her.

"I gotta go," I said, hopping up and shaking the sand out of my hair.

Ian rolled over and smiled. His arm lay across his stomach, like he didn't have a care. "No, you don't. It's earlier than you think."

I ran up to the rocks to get my shoes. "It's dawn. I have to walk Tinker Bell."

His eyelids flew open. "The Queen's dog?"

"Not Peter Pan's girlfriend," I said, checking the iPhone to see if she'd called. Fortunately she hadn't. Whew!

Ian was up in a flash. "Holy crap. We gotta go."

"I thought you said last night that we had nothing to worry about, since the Queen wasn't going to send us home this late in the summer and you and I were probably not going to end up with the Dream and Do anyway."

Hopping around on one foot, trying to tie his hiking boots in midair, he said, "Don't you know, Zoe? What guys believe at night when they want to get a girl alone and what they believe in the morning are two very different things. It's like we're not even the same person." He grinned and, nearly falling over, kissed me. "Come on. I'll show you a shortcut."

We left the lake with its odd tea-colored water and the remnants of the gristmill that I'd mistaken for boulders. Crossing a brief span of grass that I'd thought was a field, we were immediately back in the scrub-pine woods not far from the Haunted Forest, probably still on Fairyland property.

"The good news is she didn't call," I said, already breathless and sweating from dodging tree branches and climbing up embankments.

"Probably because we were out of range. Check now."

Hesitantly I pulled the iPhone from my pocket. No fewer than twenty text messages—starting at midnight and ending about five minutes ago. A wave of sickness swept over me.

"I'm doomed." The purple palace peeked through the trees of the Haunted Forest. "I went out after curfew into the Forbidden Zone and then spent the night there with a fellow cast member who, oh yeah, is a boy."

Ian stopped me right at the edge of the forest. "Was it worth it?"

I searched his dark, smiling eyes, his messy hair filled with sand, the way his mouth turned up at the corners like he was always on the verge of a laugh, and said, "You bet."

Tinker Bell was gone!

I searched everywhere in her private boudoir, even under her cashmere doggy bed and behind her crystal water bowl. Nada. What really had me worried was that her leash was still hanging on its gold hook by the door, so she had to be near.

That's when the door opened and the Queen walked

in with Tink in her arms. She took one look at me in my dirty shorts and with my unkempt hair and said, "Oh. No."

"Nothing happened. I swear!" I reached for Tink, but the Queen flinched.

"You don't deserve to hold her after what Tinksy went through, buzzing me in desperation, my poor sweet baby." She planted a kiss on Tinker Bell's head, and Tink yawned, sticking out her tiny pink tongue. "I am so disappointed, Zoe."

I hung my head. "I know. It was wrong."

"How many times have I told you never, ever, ever to . . ."

. . . *go into the Forbidden Zone.*

". . . turn off your telephonic device?" She gently placed Tinker Bell in her bed. "Honestly, Zoe, after all your weeks in my employ, I assumed it was understood that, as I have said, you are to be at my beck and call. Did you simply forget?"

"I made a mistake." I couldn't believe Ian and I were going to get away with this.

"And now look at you. Because you didn't have your telephonic device activated, you've overslept and look worse than Rumpelstiltskin on a three-day bender." She brushed her hands together as if just seeing me in this state made her feel dirty. "Well, you had better shower and change into a nice dress."

I jerked up my head. Nice dress was bad. Nice dress wasn't a gown. Nice dress meant that she was packing me back to Bridgewater. "Am I being fired?"

The Queen squinted. "What did you say?"

"Fired. Are you canning me? Like you did to Adele."

"First of all, I did not fire Adele. I demoted her to a Class B intern. Adele fired herself by running away. Second, why would I fire you?" Her gaze, cold and hard, bore straight into my soul, and it occurred to me that she would have made an excellent torturer during the Spanish Inquisition.

I willed myself to lie. "You would fire me for not being at your beck and call."

"No, dear girl. It was stupid, inconsiderate, and thoughtless, but it wasn't like you, oh, I don't know, spent the night in the Forbidden Zone."

I nearly fainted on the spot.

Was she messing with me? She had to be, because the Queen gave me a sly smile and turned to go before abruptly stopping at the door. "Oh, by the way, speaking of Adele, it may give you some comfort to know that she is well and unharmed and in close proximity to the Fairyland campus."

"How did you find out?" I asked, bracing for the worst.

The Queen placed her skeletal fingers on the door-knob. "Because I received a letter from her yesterday detailing everything." Her lips pursed in some sinister victory. "And I mean *everything*."

With that, Her Majesty left and went down the hall, her cackles ricocheting off the bare white walls.

Twenty-three

The one nice dress I had with me was a white eyelet cotton sleeveless number I'd thrown in my bag at the last minute and only because Jess, who was definitely old-school when it came to stuff like thank-you notes and avoiding blue eye shadow, had insisted that a new dress was absolutely necessary for the summer, even at a fairy-tale theme park.

"You never know," I remember her telling me as she'd sat on my bed back home in Bridgewater.

Left unspoken was the sad implication that had I had a mother around, this was the kind of womanly secret I would have learned, along with the importance of a well-made supportive bra and SPF 30 sunscreen.

With my brown hair up, my feet in a pair of cute canvas wedges, my ears accessorized with a favorite pair of crystal owl earrings, and my lips lightly glossed in shimmering pink, I was the epitome of what Jess called "Jersey ingenue."

If the Queen did indeed plan on demanding I explain Jake the Hansel's grievance—which I'm positive was in Adele's letter—or what I was doing out all night with Ian, then at least I would appear as pure as the driven snow.

Ian. I grinned at my reflection in the full-length mirror. If only he could see me now. . . .

A half hour later, right on time, I arrived with the Queen's usual tray and newspapers to find her standing on a stool, her skirts gathered about her knees, yapping in German.

"Ya, ya," the Queen was saying. *"Wir sind bereit."*

I couldn't understand a word. I pointed to the teapot, but Her Majesty indicated she didn't want any. This was serious. I'd never known the Queen not to take her Earl Grey.

"Ich verstehe. Sie können eine Zusammenkunft nicht festlegen."

Ah, German, I thought. And then . . . *Aghhh, German*! The Germans oversaw Fairyland. Heck. They *owned* Fairyland. Which meant that in effect they owned all of us, even the Queen.

"*Guten Tag. Auf Wiedersehen.*" She hung up, and Andy, who'd been cowering in the corner, rushed to her side. "What did they say?"

"That by the end of the day, we had better sign Sage to a two-year contract as our spokesperson or . . ." She closed her eyes briefly. "There it is."

"No, ma'am," Andy said. "It's gone. Maintenance came and trapped it."

I put down the tray. "What is it?"

"A mouse," the Queen hissed.

"*A* mouse?" I scanned the floor for a scurrying rodent and then, recalling the Queen's paranoia. "Or *the* Mouse?"

Andy gave me a funny look and said flatly, "A mouse has been spotted, Zoe. As I've said, Maintenance trapped it and took it away."

"They most certainly did not!" the Queen bellowed. "It's still here. It's after me. It wants to nip at my heels."

I was tempted to climb a chair, since I wasn't exactly a big fan of tiny rodents with sharp teeth myself, but when the Queen was distracted by something on one of the monitors, Andy made a point of catching my eye, shaking his head ever so slightly, and mouthing, *No mouse,* as he twirled his finger by his head in the universal pantomime for crazy.

Could it be that the Queen was under so much pressure

from the Germans that she was seeing imaginary mice?

Sugar! That's what was called for. Dashing to the tray, I stirred her maple-syrup-laced blueberries into a tablespoon of fat-free plain yogurt. "Ma'am," I said, offering it up to her since she refused to budge from her stool.

"Not this morning, Zoe. I am brunching with Mr. Adams and his manager, Michelle."

I lowered the bowl. "He's here?"

She checked her official Fairyland watch featuring Cinderella and the castle clock. "Scheduled to arrive in our underground garage at ten-oh-five."

So that was why the Queen had asked me to dress in civilian clothes, not because I was being fired, but because this was my day to escort Sage Adams. *The* Sage Adams. My heart fluttered with relief and the thrill of spending the day with a real-live celebrity—even if his music sucked.

Wait! I needed to call Sergei at the resort and let him know, so the staff would open the windows in room 505 and bring up the special lilies Michelle had requested, the ones that filtered the air. Was the Italian spring water on ice? There was so much to do!

"Then I need to get ready." Setting aside the blueberries and yogurt, I ran to get my itinerary in the Sage Adams file that, for the purposes of secrecy, I had kind of anagrammed into "Dam Sages."

The Queen halted me with the outstretched palm of her hand. "Not quite yet, Zoe. There is no telling how this morning's negotiations will fare. As much as I eagerly want to sign Sage Adams to be our spokesperson, I've ridden the merry-go-round enough to know it doesn't always go the right way.

"Therefore, I will need you to stand by for my call. Andy has arranged for an emergency backup to play Red Riding Hood for you if all goes well and, perchance, Mr. Adams is interested in touring the park after brunch. Meanwhile I need you to do a search through my files, Zoe." She smiled thinly. *"All. Five. Boxes."*

This was my punishment for being late to walk Tinker Bell—sorting through five boxes of files.

Her smile grew wider. "In the basement."

The basement! That dingy, damp place with the spiders and centipedes and silverfish? Oh, crud.

"Tsk, tsk. Don't look so dismayed," she said, gingerly stepping off her stool. "This time, however, please do remember to keep your telephonic device activated. Would be such a shame if I couldn't reach you to escort Mr. Adams, and I had to rely on someone like Valerie."

The assignment couldn't have been more dreary: to find a five-page memo from the Germans about something called PUD:1,001 that Evelyn had accidentally archived in storage.

The PUD:1,001 boxes were in the vault where all the important Fairyland documents were kept. I would need my master key and also a special combination that the Queen gave me to use on a lock behind a false basement thermostat. Which meant I would be spending a sunny August morning locked away in a windowless room searching through papers, away from everyone. Away from Ian.

There, I said it.

On the off chance I might run into him during breakfast, I stopped by the cafeteria to grab something to eat, since I was starved and it wasn't like there was a vending machine in the basement. Jess and RJ were hanging out drinking coffee, and when she saw me, Jess practically leaped across tables to make sure I was alive by squeezing me to death.

"I was so worried." She gave me another hug. "I stopped by your room this morning and knocked to see if you wanted to meet up for coffee. I figured you were out walking Tink, but when I came back a half hour later you still weren't there or in the bathroom. I worried that maybe you never made it back from You-Know-Where last night."

"I'm fine," I said, doing a quick check for Ian. No sign. Bummer.

Jess insisted I sit down and tell her everything over pancakes. As RJ showed no signs of excusing himself from the table, I had to omit the best part of my story, about spending the night with Ian. That, RJ definitely would have had to report.

I poured on a dab more maple syrup. "So now she's ordered me to the basement to search through five boxes of files with an ominous name like PUD:1,001 to find some progress report." I licked my finger and recapped the bottle.

Jess wrinkled her nose. "One thousand and one files?"

"Let's hope not," I said, realizing that I was famished after missing dinner the night before.

RJ, who'd been silently listening to our conversation, said, "I don't get why you're being punished if all you did was accidentally turn off the Queen's cell."

I shrugged. "She tried to reach me all night, and then she had to wake up early and walk Tinker Bell. That's why she's pissed."

Jess bit her lip, and I could tell she was worried this meant I'd disqualified myself from the Dream & Do.

"I've given up," I said. "There's no way I'm gonna get the Dream and Do. I'm not a princess. I picked Her Majesty's precious flowers my first day on the job. And now this."

RJ leaned forward. "So why do you even try to please her?"

It was a valid question, and I didn't answer it off the

cuff. I thought about it. "Because I don't want Jess to be a victim of guilt by association. . . ."

Jess said, "Right. Like you haven't single-handedly made my summer by pulling strings to make me Cinderella."

I ignored that. "And because there's still a chance I'm in the running. And as long as there's still a chance, I'm going to keep on trying."

My cousin turned to RJ. "What do you think? Is she still okay?"

RJ's fingers played with a straw on the table as he scrutinized me under his heavy black brows. "From the rumors I've been hearing in the front office, Zoe's doing fine."

But he wasn't looking where I was looking. RJ was looking at me, and I was looking at Dash, who was jerking his thumb toward the hall. Apparently we had to chat.

Goody.

Twenty-four

"I stopped by your room last night hoping we could talk and maybe you could show me that you really had the shirt swatch," he said. "I sat outside your door for an hour. Where were you?"

"Gee, Mom, no need to wait up," I said, heading toward the elevators. "By the way, you being in the girls' dorm after ten is a violation of the Fairyland rules, you know. Number six, to be exact. That would seriously harm your chances of winning the Dream and Do were the Queen to find out."

A couple of furries passed on their way to get into position for the park opening in about ten minutes. Dash, exasperated by my insouciance, almost ran his fingers through his newly sprayed princely hairdo and caught himself from messing it up in the nick of time.

"I don't know where all this hostility is coming from," he said earnestly. "I'm being honest about what happened so I can save Marcus's rep. I'm trying to do the stand-up thing here."

"Except you're not." I eyed him levelly, curious as to whether he'd flinch. "It's not your shirt. You weren't the one who saved me from the quicksand. You and I never met in the Forbidden Zone, ever."

"What?"

"You heard me. You're trying to set me up." Don't back down, Zoe.

"How could you say that?" He shook his head, confused, as if no one had ever accused him of something so hurtful and I, being a sucker for boys on the verge of tears, almost bought it until I remembered that Dash Merrill had spent summers at acting camps and probably school years on the stage as well. His pleading frown, those puppy-dog eyes, were nothing but the product of lots of training. I even wondered if the heartbreaking story about his father laying on the guilt had been bogus, too.

"Okay, if I wasn't the guy you saw in the Forbidden Zone, then who was?" Dash had smoothly shifted into playing the part of righteous prosecutor.

It just so happened that Ian chose that moment to come down the hall with two other princes on their way to the stables. Seeing me, he lit up with that winning grin of his, and I couldn't resist going all tingly. On any other guy, that Prince Charming costume was dork galore, but on him it was seriously sexy.

"Hey, Zoe. You look awesome, but what's with the dress? Not working today?" He turned to Dash and did that guy-grunt thing, nodding his chin. "Hey."

Dash nodded back. "Hey."

Ian said, "What's up?"

"Just talking." Dash backed off, the chicken.

"Doesn't seem like you're just talking. Seems like something's going on. You okay, Zoe?"

I rolled my eyes. "Of course. It's nothing." Though I could tell that Ian suspected Dash was again trying to force me to come clean to the Queen.

Dash slid his gaze from Ian to me and back to Ian again, gauging our reaction, adding two and two. The first buzzer buzzed, the cue for everyone to get in their places. Ian and Dash would have to run, since the stables were a good mile of hallway off.

"See ya later?" Ian asked, finding my hand.

I closed my eyes. *Don't. Dash will use it against us!*

It was too late. Ian cupped my face and kissed me in front of everyone, including Dash. When we broke apart,

Dash was giving an evil smile, a threat that said: *I'm gonna make sure you two get yourselves so disqualified.*

There was nothing I could do about Dash, and Dash couldn't do anything about us, not as long as he was in the park playing Prince Charming to Valerie's Sleeping Beauty. So I shoved my worries aside and got on with life.

After the first-shift cast members left for the park, I took the elevator in Our World to the basement, which was two levels below ground, damp, and cold. I'd been to the file room only once before, to fetch a box of purchase orders, but I'd never been in the vault, where the really important papers were kept. And, being slightly claustrophobic, I'd never had any burning desire to go there, either.

The door to the vault looked like your average supply closet, which I opened with my master key. Inside, however, a combination lock hidden behind a false thermostat opened a steel door. After I unlocked that, I flicked on a light switch and sighed. Floor-to-ceiling metal shelves crammed with boxes, five of which, at eye level, were marked PUD:1,001.

I started with box number one and flipped through each page, keeping an eye out for what the Queen described as a progress report from our parent company,

Die Über Wunderbar, on official corporate stationery marked July 25.

It actually didn't take as long as I'd feared. The memo was right on top. I gave it a quick read to make sure I'd found the right one.

As far as I was able to glean, PUD:1,001 stood for the proposed 1,001 Nights Theme Park & Adventure Land, a huge Fairyland expansion plan aimed at attracting "mature teenagers and young adults" with "thrill-a-minute" rides that were sure to "brand" Fairyland Kingdom as a destination spot for theme-park enthusiasts worldwide.

I definitely wasn't supposed to be reading this, but I couldn't stop. I mean, a theme park based on *The Arabian Nights*? It was brilliant! I especially loved the names of the "anchor" attractions and their ridiculous, hyperbolic characterizations.

SINBAD'S SEVEN DEADLY SEAS: 1 boat. 30
seats. 100 Terrorizing Waves. As close to experiencing
the perfect storm without heading into the open ocean.
Through the magic of modern technology, guests face
imminent peril, as for 6 terrifying minutes the boat
lists in both directions, submerges, and finally capsizes.
(*Not suitable for those with heart conditions, nervous
disorders, epilepsy, or weak stomachs. Guests must be
age 16 or older.)

ALI BABA'S 40 THIEVES: Think Prince of Persia was challenging? Try fighting 40 armed thieves in a closed-door cave for real. At stake, all the gold you can handle . . . and your life. (*Not suitable for those with heart conditions, nervous disorders, epilepsy, or weak stomachs. Guests must be age 16 or older.)

ALADDIN'S MAGIC CARPET RIDE: Guaranteed to impress even the most die-hard roller-coaster enthusiasts, Aladdin's Magic Carpet Ride will circumnavigate the 1,001 Park with its 4,000-foot track thrilling guests with two 90-degree plunges and 20-foot-tall drops while reaching speeds in excess of 75 miles per hour. This alone will put the 1,001 NIGHTS THEME PARK & ADVENTURE LAND in the Guinness Book of World Records. (*Not suitable for those with heart conditions, nervous disorders, epilepsy, or weak stomachs. Guests must be age 16 or older.)

SCHEHERAZADE'S FINAL TWIST: Prepare to scream for mercy as a hydraulic launch sends you hurling at 90 miles per hour through a corkscrew coaster. While the ride lasts only 60 seconds, it will seem like an eternity with four 360-degree rotations. (*Not suitable for those with heart conditions, nervous disorders, epilepsy, or weak stomachs. Guests must be age 16 or older.)

That was only the beginning. In addition a holographic genie would emerge from a magic lamp if rubbed, and a new Ali's Palace, "grander and more ornate than any palace in Fairyland Kingdom's history," would situate the new park in a "Mecca of Persian magnificence" surrounded by open market stalls selling rugs, fabrics, silks, home furnishings, and jewelry "heretofore found only in such exotic realms as Morocco for Morocco market prices."

Final architectural and development plans were in the drafting stages, though "confidential inquiries for permitting" had begun. There was a lot of incredibly dull stuff about environmental impacts on the surrounding Pinelands—this, apparently, had been holding up the works—and how that could be avoided by designating other undeveloped Fairyland properties as permanent wetlands and/or nature preserves.

I quickly glanced at a map and was surprised to see how much of the Pinelands Fairyland had owned: thousands of acres, before the woods were designated as a National Reserve. From my rough assessment, the theme park would go right where Ian and I had spent the night, at the old gristmill—which was too bad, as that place was awesome.

I'd just finished reading the report when the Queen's iPhone blared "Every Breath You Take."

She sounded ebullient. "Joyous tidings, Zoe. Stop what you're doing, wash your hands, brush your teeth, regloss your lips, and meet us at the ground floor of the Princess Palace with your best face forward. Our brunch was supremely productive."

I asked her what she ate, but she ignored me. Food for her was always beside the point.

"Suffice to say, we are this close from forging an agreement. Mr. Adams has essentially uttered a verbal contract, and his lawyers are reviewing the final paperwork as we speak. All we need to do is quickly show him the park in the interim and, after a quick jaunt through the Haunted Forest, the spokesmanship papers will be waiting for him to sign when he returns."

Unreal. Somehow the Queen had managed the impossible—she had hooked Sage Adams, thereby saving her job and quite possibly the park.

"Congratulations!" I exclaimed. "Are foie gras and champagne in Tinker Bell's future?"

"Tut, tut. Don't jinx it. Just be here in two shakes of Bo Peep's lamb's tail. Mr. Adams and his, um, manager, do not wish to be kept waiting."

Who does? I wondered as I locked the vault and exited the file room, closing it securely behind me. Then I ran down the hall toward the elevator, where, for some reason, RJ was standing reading a book.

"You got a minute?" he asked, tucking the book under his arm.

I didn't. If this was about Jess and him, his love life would have to take a number. "Sorry, RJ," I said, slipping the Die Über Wunderbar progress report into my bag. "The Queen needs me upstairs right away."

"No, she doesn't." He moved in front of the buttons so I couldn't reach them.

"RJ," I tried, trying to push him aside, anxious to get going. "This is serious."

"So is this." He was steadfast, like a slab of granite, and unsmiling. It was as though the laid-back, all-knowing, wise RJ—who'd advised us to avoid Chef's Surprise and had stuck out his neck for me by leaning on a former lady-in-waiting for tips on how to please the Queen—was gone. In his place was a guy I didn't recognize.

"When you mentioned that the Queen had sent you down here to go through the PUD:1,001 files, I knew I'd found the solution. Zoe, you need to give me that progress report so I can show it to the Mouse."

I was not in the mood for pranks. The Queen needed me. "Quit kidding around. I don't have time for this." I tried slipping my hand over his shoulder to press the button, but he grabbed my wrist and held it tightly.

"Here's the truth, Zoe: I didn't come back to Fairyland this summer to work my way up the corporate ladder.

When I was an intern last year, I got wind that they were planning to expand into the Pinelands, and I decided I would do everything in my power to prevent that from happening."

He let go, and I had to shake my arm to stop it from tingling. Was he messing with me? RJ was Mr. Fairyland, the star former intern who knew the rules and lectured me to learn them, too. This couldn't be for real.

"I won't go into all the environmental degradation they'll inflict with this expansion, but trust me when I tell you the damage will be permanent and severe. Rare forms of amphibians, birdlife, and reptiles like the spike-nosed hornbeam turtle will lose their nesting grounds. I was outraged, and you should be, too."

"I'm sure I will be outraged," I said. "Right now, I need to—"

"Give me the report."

Please, this was getting ridiculous. "Are we done now?"

"The Mouse is the only one that can stop the project," he said. "Fairyland's their closest competition, and, for the most part, a pretty wimpy one. But it will move heaven and earth to make sure Fairyland doesn't expand."

We exchanged stares, and I saw this wasn't a prank. RJ was being totally straight. He really was outraged by the 1,001 project, and he really wanted the plans that were currently burning a hole in my bag.

Every breath you take . . .

I shuddered and snatched my phone.

"Where are you, Zoe? This is embarrassing." The Queen was beyond peeved.

"Coming!" I slid the phone to Off. "RJ, I've got to—"

He took the phone out of my hand and started inputting numbers. "Here," he said, handing it back to me. "This is the number to my secret cell phone. If you change your mind, call me, and I'll take care of everything."

I gaped at what he'd done. "I can't believe you just did that. Do you know what will happen if the Queen sees this? She'll stroke out." I tried deleting it but couldn't. RJ must have locked it somehow.

"The Queen is not your friend, Zoe."

"Uh-huh." I started riffling through my bag looking for a hairbrush or lip gloss. If RJ wasn't going to let me pass, then at least I could make myself presentable until he did. "The Queen might not be my friend, but she's treated me just fine. Look, as a favor to me, she made Jess a princess!"

RJ chuckled knowingly. "As if that matters. To the Queen, Jess is a joke, and so are you—except that you're a joke who does her bidding, which is why she keeps you on. When you're gone she laughs behind your back at how she can make you do anything she wants with just the snap of her fingers."

I slapped my hands over my ears, wishing he would quit saying all these nasty things. The Queen was a tough customer, sure, but deep down I liked to believe she had a good soul.

"She wants you to think that you're in the running for the Dream and Do, but that's a lie," RJ continued. "She knew from the get-go who was going to win. . . ."

I quit brushing. "Dash and Valerie?"

He nodded. "Dash and Valerie have been bred for Fairyland corporate since they were children. They're out for themselves, and they don't give a damn about who they have to step on to get ahead. Not like you, Zoe. You look out for Jess, and Jess loves you. It's touching, your relationship. That's why you two don't stand a chance. You guys are too soft."

It can't be true, I thought, so unnerved that I was getting a headache. I didn't even hear my phone blaring "Every Breath You Take" over and over again until RJ plucked it out of my hand and put it on mute.

"Look, as soon as I have that report, I'll call the Mouse, and within an hour a limo will arrive to whisk you away from here. You and Jess will be compensated with double the Dream and Do money so that Jess can go to college and you can pay off your mom's medical bills. In the process you'll have saved a precious part of the Pinelands for generations of wildlife to come, while sending a message to Fairyland and the Queen that they can take their corporate mind games and shove 'em."

He handed me back the phone. It felt cold and hard and, suddenly, powerful.

"It's the right thing to do," RJ said softly. "And you, Zoe Kiefer, are the right person to do it."

Twenty-five

The Queen greeted me with her warmest smile yet. "Ah, here is my loyal assistant," she announced as I rushed from the elevator to where the group was assembled.

She slid an arm around my shoulder, and I felt repulsed.

She laughs behind your back at how she can make you do anything she wants with just the snap of her fingers.

Those words kept playing over and over in my mind like a bad Billy Joel song in the mall. My headache was growing worse.

"I'm sorry I'm late," I mumbled. "I was held up."

"We'll discuss it later," she murmured out of the side of her mouth. "Meanwhile, Zoe, I'd like you to meet our two most special guests." She cleared her throat as a reminder that I was under no circumstances to use Sage's real name in public. "This is Michelle."

Michelle, who was on her cell, was a rather frumpy woman with brassy, red corkscrew hair who'd made the unfortunate choice to wear all black on this sweltering day. She waved a finger and rudely kept on talking.

"And this," the Queen said, directing me to a guy in aviator sunglasses, a Phillies baseball cap, black T-shirt, super-skinny jeans, and his signature red-and-black-striped scarf that he'd worn during every one of his *American Idol* appearances, "is our VIP."

Sage Adams. *The* Sage Adams. Even though I was not a fan, I couldn't help but be so starstruck that all the horrible things RJ had said about Fairyland faded away.

He took my hand and in a super-sexy voice said, "I'm Sage. You are?"

"You're not supposed to say," I blurted out.

He tilted his head. "Now that's an interesting name. I thought you'd be more like a Jane or an Ashley. . . ."

"Zoe." God. What was wrong with me? *Get a grip.* "My name is Zoe, but we're not supposed to say yours."

"Ah, yes." He dropped my hand and thumbed toward Michelle. "That would be Mother's suggestion."

So Michelle was his mother, and from the looks of her, a holy terror. She and the Queen probably got along like peas in a pod.

"Shall we proceed?" the Queen suggested. "Don't keep them out long, Zoe. It's a hot day, and I'm sure our VIPs would like to enjoy all the amenities of our fine resort after such a spectacular performance last night in . . . Where was it again?"

Sage said, "Boise. Boise, Idaho." He grinned. "Potatoes, you know."

And despite the Queen's disapproving glare, I giggled. Well, she'd only be laughing at me later, I decided. Who cares?

Sage, Michelle, and I headed out into the bright light, and I knew without asking that guests were noticing our odd troupe. Sage—in his "celebrity casual" outfit of hat and sunglasses and the telltale red-and-black wool scarf—would be a paparazzi magnet while Michelle, whose hair in the sunlight shone a brilliant orange, huffed and barked orders into her cell.

Sweat began to bead between my shoulder blades even though I was wearing the equivalent of cotton Kleenex. I headed toward the Haunted Forest, where it was shadier.

"I thought we'd start off with the underground roller coaster in the Seven Dwarfs' Mine and end on Mr. Toad's Wild Slide," I said, though I doubted Sage had brought his swimsuit.

"This is inexcusable," Michelle crowed behind us. "I will not agree to those terms."

I thought she was referring to the tour and was relieved to find she was yelling at someone on her phone. Valerie and Dash strolled by in costume holding hands. I thought I saw a flicker of recognition in Valerie's eyes when she saw Sage in his scarf. If not recognition, then an instinctual awareness that he was someone different and that I, in my civilian clothes, was different, too.

"Do you know them?" Sage asked.

"Of course. There are only forty of us in the program."

Sage went, "*Hmm*. Lots of drama?"

I thought I wasn't supposed to be conversing, but I said anyway, "You have no idea."

He laughed.

We got to the Seven Dwarfs' Mine, where I flashed my badge and moved Sage to the front of the line. Several people who'd been waiting for probably more than a half hour grumbled, and I had to placate them with coupons for free ice cream. Sage stepped to the first cart, and Gary, a troll on duty, reminded him to remove the scarf.

"But then my head will fall off," Sage quipped.

I should have told him that trolls were not exactly famous for their humor. "You'll be a guy strung up by his neck if you don't give me that scarf," the troll said.

Sage gave him a salute and unwrapped the scarf.

I'd forgotten how scary that ride was, especially with all the flashing lights and sudden drops. My stomach, already in turmoil from my run-ins with Dash and RJ, didn't appreciate the upside-down parts, either. But when I looked over to Sage, I found him with his chin in his chest, asleep. He woke only at the end, when the train surfaced to arrive at Snow White's Cottage.

"My. That was thrilling." He yawned.

I said, "You're pretty tired, aren't you?"

"After performing in twenty cities in as many days, you'd be, too."

I guess I hadn't thought that being famous would be grueling. It seemed like so much fun. All the attention, the photographers, the clothes, and the parties. But here was Sage practically sleepwalking, and I was half tempted to tell him to forget the tour and just go back to the hotel room.

Michelle was waiting on the platform, still on her phone. "It's a matter of the right branding," she barked. "The question is: Do we want Sage associated with a theme park that has seen better days?"

Yowza!

"I think this is a fine little theme park," Sage said, by way of apology. "I wish I could live here."

His condescending tone rubbed me so wrong that, despite my current lack of Wow!™ spirit, I ruffled in defense. "Actually it's a pretty cool place."

Sage smiled thinly. "I'm sure it is, if you say so."

A couple of witches jumped out at us from trees, and Sage duly pretended to be scared. We passed Hansel and Gretel's Candy Cottage, where we broke off candy from the fence and watched Red Riding Hood and the Wolf.

"I don't get why the Wolf is carrying a purse," Sage said.

"Because he's a grandmother."

"Yeah, but he's in a nightgown. And how come he's in heels?"

I started to laugh, but Michelle poked my back. "Not so close," she hissed. "My client needs his space."

I could see Sage roll his eyes beneath his aviators. I took a couple of steps to the right just to be polite, but Sage whispered, "Don't listen to her. I call the shots."

I snuck a glance at Michelle, all puffed up over being a big shot in the entertainment world, and felt vague disgust for the way she was exploiting her son. Before Sage's *American Idol* success, Michelle had probably been one of those stage moms dragging him from audition to audition, and now that he'd won some success she was determined to cash in on every last bit of his fame.

Just then Ian galloped across the green and leaped from his horse to come to Red Riding Hood's rescue. Seeing me with Sage, he cocked his head in curiosity and then recited his standard line: "Is there a problem, good maidens?"

"Who is that?" Sage asked.

"Ian Davidson," I said levelly. "He's one of the Prince Charmings."

"No kidding." Sage waited a beat. "I can tell he's charmed you."

My cheeks went hot, and I reminded myself to be professional. "We're friends."

"If I were Prince Charming, I'd be your friend, too," he said, loud enough for his mother to hear. He slid an arm around me and winked.

I knew he just wanted to piss off Michelle, which was why I didn't shrug him off, though I wished I had, because at that moment he pushed it too far, planting his lips firmly on mine . . .

. . . right in front of Ian.

It all happened so fast, yet in slow motion, too. There was Sage with his arm around me, moving in for a kiss, and then there was Ian gaping at us in disbelief.

I pushed Sage away. "Not funny."

Michelle got off her phone. "How dare you!"

"It was nothing," said Sage, though I couldn't tell if he was referring to his kiss or my push.

Ian glared at Sage. For all Ian knew, Sage was an old boyfriend, and that's why I was in civilian clothes. He had no idea that Sage was a celebrity VIP and that I was just doing my job.

Completely stepping out of character, Ian left the Red Riding Hood set, dismounted his horse, and strode toward us. "Something you forgot to tell me, Zoe?" he asked angrily, giving Sage a dirty look.

Sage bowed. "If I have offended thy good prince by kissing his fair wench, then I apologize."

I winced. Cinderella's Prince Charming was only supposed to have one *wench*—Cinderella—and I prayed no kid had been close enough to hear. Fortunately, Jess was working in the park and, having caught wind of the growing tension, had moved swiftly across Fiddler's Green to my rescue.

As were Dash and Valerie, who was whispering excitedly, probably because she'd recognized Sage. Dash, meanwhile, was grinning and not in a good way. It was the same evil grin he got when Ian kissed me.

What happened next took, at most, ten seconds, but it seemed like hours as everything exploded when I said to Ian, "He's just a friend."

Ian said sarcastically, "I can see that."

Jess arrived breathless, right when Sage whipped off his sunglasses. She would have blurted, "Oh my god! You're Sage Adams!" if I hadn't given her *the Look*.

"We're on Fairyland business," I said, under my breath. "On the down low."

Michelle got off her phone. "What's going on here?"

Dash unhooked himself from the gawking Valerie and slapped Ian on the back. "Don't take it so hard, bro. You're not the only one to get screwed over by Zoe. She hooks up with every guy here."

If Ian hadn't swung around and socked him in the jaw, I would have. All it took was one hard blow from Ian's fist and Dash teetered backward like a Weeble and went down for the count, a Prince Charming in his noble navy coat laid out on the green. The trolls came running, along with Karl in his wolf costume.

Valerie screamed. Sage said, "Wow! Impressive," while Jess cursed, "You freaking liar!" and gave Dash a kick with her faux glass slipper.

Michelle yanked me to her side and tore off her sunglasses to reveal beady eyes rimmed in bloodred. "You have just totally blown it, Lady-in-Waiting. Take me to the front office, so I can personally inform your boss that this deal is dead."

Twenty-six

I was fired.

"The facts are indisputable. You allowed a situation to get out of control, and because of that we lost the opportunity to sign on Sage Adams as our spokesman." The Queen reclined in her chair and petted Tinker Bell, who was snuggling in her lap. I expected they would both be looking for new quarters after this summer, since Her Majesty's long tenure as overseer of Fairyland had ended with Ian's single punch.

"You have displayed a shocking lack of Wow! spirit."

That really got to me, even though I'd been telling myself nothing mattered, that the Queen thought I was a simpering lackey for whom she had no respect. The sad truth was that I had come to like the Queen. Not in a cozy, best-friend way, but in the way you'd appreciate a chemistry teacher who's been hard on you all year and, as a result, you ace the AP chem exam because you really do understand covalent bonds.

"There are steps that must be taken," she said, placing Tinker Bell back on her doggy bed. "Though Michelle has made it evident that no contract will be in the offing, simple courtesy, Zoe, requires you to appear at Mr. Adams's room with an apology and an explanation."

I failed to see how this was entirely my fault. If anything, competition for the Dream and Do grant was to blame, since it brought out the worst in us. Ian wasn't a violent guy, and maybe, in another setting, Dash wasn't a total jerk. I certainly wasn't the type to play two guys off each other at once, and if Jess had ever kicked, punched, or in any way physically harmed anyone before, it was news to me.

Still, because I'd been so well-trained, I said, "Yes, ma'am."

"Then you are to return to your room, pack your bags, and make arrangements to be transported to the bus station tomorrow morning, which is when you will also relinquish your master key and the telephonic device that I have trustingly placed in your possession."

The phone was in the pocket of my dress with RJ's number just begging to be pressed. Once the Queen was finished with me, I could use it to call him and tell him to get the PUD:1,001 progress report that was still in my bag, since I'd been too busy with Sage and his mother to deliver it to the Queen. How sweet would it be to pull out of Fairyland fifty thousand dollars richer in a big black stretch limousine?

So long, suckers!

I said, "Yes, ma'am. I will pack, make arrangements for the bus, and turn over the key and phone tomorrow."

"I may still require your services in the interim."

I nodded.

She flicked me off with her fingers. "Be gone."

The door slid open, and I was excused. Evelyn at her desk regarded me over her half glasses. "I'm so sorry it ended this way, Zoe."

"So am I." What else was there to say? Everything I'd worked so hard for—including Jess's role as Cinderella— was a total bust.

I headed for the resort and to room 505. My only hope was that Michelle was out, because she was the last person I wanted to face. What a horrid, horrid woman.

Taking a deep breath, I knocked on the door. "It's me, Zoe. Your escort."

I waited as someone came to the door. When it opened I was relieved to see it was Sage in a gray T-shirt and jeans. Reading my mind, he said, "Don't worry. She's not here. Come in."

He waved me in, and I stepped inside feeling slightly nervous. After his performance in the park, I wasn't sure what to expect.

"My apologies." He clapped his hands together prayerfully. "I was trying to annoy my mother and, unfortunately, other people were harmed."

I appreciated the sentiment, even if it was too late and directed at the wrong person. "Actually I was sent here to apologize to you."

Sage shook his head and sighed. "Adults. I mean, what can you say?"

I smiled as he opened the fridge that I had personally stocked with all sorts of expensive water and organic fruit juices to see he'd slipped in two Cokes. Cracking one open, he handed it to me sheepishly. "All that other stuff's for show. I'm a total sugar addict."

We moved over to the table by the window that, incidentally, Sage had opened, despite the threat of paparazzi. I didn't really know what my role was here. I'd apologized. I'd been fired. I was done.

But Sage insisted on reminiscing about Fairyland and how it had a special place in his heart because his family used to go to Storytown when he was a kid, before he got famous. Before his parents got divorced and Michelle turned into the stage-manager mother from hell.

"Believe it or not, Mom used to take me here all the

time when we were living outside Philly. She was like a big kid back then, loving Storytown as much as I did," he said, resting his chin on his hand and gazing wistfully toward the park. "That's why when I heard Fairyland wanted to make me a spokesperson, I was all gung ho, though Mom's theory is that Fairyland's best years are behind it. All the more reason, if you ask me."

I was telling Sage how much Storytown had meant to me, too, when there was another knock at the door, followed by Ian's voice. At the sound of it, my heart seized.

Sage whispered, "It'll be okay."

When Ian walked in, Sage held up his arms. "Don't hit me."

"I am sorry, man," Ian said, extending his hand to shake Sage's. "I came here to apologize. I acted like a jerk."

"Forget it," Sage said. "I was the one who started it. Unfortunately Zoe's paying the price."

Ian must not have noticed I was there, because as soon as he caught sight of me over Sage's shoulder, his eyes shone with regret. "Oh, Zoe, I don't know what to say."

"Tell her you like her," Sage said. "She obviously likes you."

More embarrassment. I bowed my head as Ian came over and, kneeling next to me, repeated a line from his "audition" that day in the Queen's office. "I am the worst guy ever."

"No, you're not." In fact, secretly, I was kind of touched that he'd defended my honor. "Besides, Dash had it coming."

Ian grinned. "Is all forgiven, dearest?" Complete with batting eyes, another repeat performance.

Again I couldn't help but laugh.

"It was my fault!" Sage exclaimed. "Do you want me to do something? Call your boss?"

I said, "Agree to be the spokesperson."

Sage slumped. "That I cannot do. Unfortunately, until I turn eighteen, my mother has control."

So that was it. There was no solution. When I told Ian I'd been fired, he slapped his forehead and cursed.

"Too bad we can't go back to Storytown and go through the Way Back Machine, eh, Zoe?" Sage asked, referring to a perennial Storytown favorite, an attraction where you could "go back in time," even though all you did was walk through a sewer pipe lined with black-and-white spiraled rope lights—that is, if you could keep from being so dizzy that you fell down.

Ian said, "Let's find out if it's still around. They put up a wall around the ruins of Storytown but you can get in if you happen to know how. Which I do."

Sage nodded. "Why not? I've got nothing else to do for the rest of the day and I'm bloody sick of hotel rooms. How about you, Zoe?"

"Sure. Why not? By tomorrow I'll be back in Bridge-water anyway."

Sage tossed his empty Coke can into the recycling bin. "Great. Let's go."

And that was that. I was about to commit the one sin the Queen had specifically requested I not do. But I suppose that's what she got for firing me and, on the bright side, at least I hadn't turned over the progress report to RJ.

Yet.

The evening parade was under way, so there wasn't anyone in the Haunted Forest when Ian, Sage, and I emerged from the secret door by the Frog Prince's Pond. Ian led the way, bushwhacking through underbrush until we found a worn path that snaked through a pine grove. Sage, in his pricey YMC suede boots, was slipping more than I was in my wedges, and he was complaining constantly. At last we came to a dark stone wall, the same wall I'd been examining when I'd fallen into the quicksand.

"You don't want to go over there." Ian pointed to some loose soil at the wall's base. "As you can see, the wall dips down. It's literally sinking. But there's a way to get in right here." He ripped down some vines to reveal a flimsy wooden door that opened with a mere push.

Sage went, "Whoa. This place is so overgrown, it's like

coming across some ruins in the jungle." He went first. "You guys have gotta see this. It is *sur-real*."

Which was his way of saying Storytown was a dump covered in weeds and littered with debris. No wonder the Queen had instructed me to keep Sage out of here at all costs, since many of the attractions had been left to simply rot.

The Old Woman's Shoe had once been bright red, I recalled, with a ladder you could climb to the top and a slide that would take you to the inside. The ladder was gone, and most of the paint had peeled away, just like the merry-go-round that in better days had glittered with gold horses and intricately designed carriages. Someone had removed the horses and seats, leaving only the center. It was uniquely depressing.

As for the Way Back Machine, it was now just a dirty old sewer pipe filled with trash, leaves, and what appeared to be broken glass.

Sage stood by Peter Peter Pumpkin Eater's oversize pumpkin, now defiled by black spray-painted graffiti that read Welcome to Zombie Land. He tossed me his cell. "Take a photo. I have to preserve this moment for posterity."

A photo like that would be proof that we'd taken Sage to Storytown, and if it was posted online, it would seriously damage Fairyland's rep. I tried explaining that to

Sage, but he insisted.

"If anything, Storytown makes me love Fairyland more," he said, posing with his arms straight out, like a zombie. "For some reason they saved it, and that tells me this park still has soul. It *needs* to be saved."

Click! I took the photo.

"Cinderella's Castle," Sage said, taking the phone back so he could shoot his own picture of the fading pink fortress that wasn't much bigger than our garage at home. "I *remember* that." He jogged off to explore what was left inside.

Ian stood at the edge of an embankment. "The moat's gone. Nothing but a ring of blue-painted concrete."

But the willow tree was still there.

A lump rose to my throat. Storytown might have decayed into rust and witchgrass, but the tree remained steadfast, as proof that once upon a time there really had been a woman who so adored her daughter that she brought her to a special place where fairy tales and nursery rhymes came true.

I let the memories flood in: Mom running ahead of me in jean shorts and a red-checked top, her ponytail bouncing behind her as she led me through Mary, Mary Quite Contrary's Garden.

I saw us paddling the swan boats, her lifting me up so I could see Cinderella on the drawbridge. Gently guiding my hand that was clutching the cracker for Little Bo Peep's sheep. I could even feel the mounting trepidation as the sheep's mouth got closer and closer and then stole the cracker from my tiny fingers.

"Mom," I whispered, hoping maybe, wherever she was, she'd hear. Even though I knew that was silly, I couldn't help it.

"Hey, what's wrong?" Ian's voice broke through my fog.

I didn't want to tell him, because how would I explain that a willow tree just made me cry?

"Did your mom used to take you here?" he asked softly.

I nodded. "It's been such a crappy day, getting fired and . . . other stuff . . . and then seeing this . . . I swear, I don't cry all the time."

He wiped away my tears with his thumbs as he had the night before when I'd broken down the first time. "Zoe, it's okay. You loved your mom, and your mom used to bring you here." He pulled me into him and rested my head on his chest. "It'd be weird if you didn't cry."

He stroked my hair and didn't say anything as I let it all out, the stress of serving the Queen, trying so hard to be perfect, and then learning that I'd been nothing but a laughingstock all along.

If I'd had a mother, she'd be there in Bridgewater

when I'd get home tomorrow to listen and understand and tell me that the Queen was a dried-up, two-bit theme-park manager. But there would be only my dad, and even though he was a sweetheart and did everything he could for me, at the end of the day he wasn't my mother.

"I should go," Ian said, after a while. "Not that I'm not loving every aspect of this." He looked down at me and smiled. "But, you know, the hot-dog-and-mac-and-cheese crowd awaits."

I sniffed back the tears and said, "Yeah. I gotta pack."

"Lemme go find Sage and tell him," Ian said. "You wait here."

While Ian crossed the drawbridge into Cinderella's Castle, I walked over to the willow and knelt at its roots, focusing on what this place meant to Mom and me. Perhaps here, right at this spot, we'd leaned against this trunk and stuck our legs out over this cool, green grass and fed the ducks. Mom would have remembered; I'd been too young.

I fingered the willow's brittle bark with the hope that by mere touch I could resurrect the past. But of course I couldn't. So I did the next best thing.

Reaching into my shirt, I removed Mom's single-pearl necklace, the one Dad had given her the day I was born, and dropped it in a small hole I dug with my finger. Patting over the dirt, I knelt there.

"I miss you, Mom." My chest ached, and so did every

muscle as I fought back another bout of sobs. I guess this was the release Ari had encouraged, the "letting go" that I didn't want to do.

It'll happen when you least expect it, he'd said at one of our last sessions. "Maybe in class or at the movies or while cleaning out your mother's closet."

Or at an abandoned nursery-rhyme theme park. *Didn't think of that, did you, Ari?*

I felt a touch and nearly leaped out of my skin, but it was only Ian.

"Sage is gonna stay here and keep looking around. You ready?" he asked, offering me his hand.

I took one last glance at the willow. Bye, Mom, I thought, running my finger over the disturbed dirt. See you later.

I stood and took Ian's hand. "Ready as I'll ever be."

Twenty-seven

I spent the last night in Fairyland hanging out at the Frog Prince's Pond with Ian and Jess and RJ, though I could barely look RJ in the eye.

There were a couple of times when I almost took Jess aside to tell her that her BF was not the dude he appeared to be. What worried me was that if he could live a lie, like being Mr. Fairyland, then what about his feelings toward Jess? RJ could have been lying about those, too.

But whenever I looked, they were holding hands or stealing quick kisses. She was obviously so freaking happy that no way was I going to be the messenger bearing bad news—and, besides, there was always the possibility that RJ really did like her. I hoped so, because Jess was too good a person to have her heart broken.

Meanwhile, Jess was irate over my shoddy treatment, since, apparently, I was the only one being punished. The Queen hadn't so much as reprimanded her, Ian, or, according to all reports, Dash. It was so unfair.

"It's because you're expendable," RJ said, when Jess and Ian were off swimming. "How does that make you feel?"

Perched on the lily pad, I hugged my knees. "How do you think it makes me feel? Like crud."

"Then why don't you give me that progress report?"

"Maybe I will," I said, still unsure of what was right. "I'm not leaving until tomorrow."

I did not want to think about tomorrow. After tomorrow I'd be in Bridgewater without Jess. Without Ian. It was a double blow.

Jess and RJ thoughtfully went on ahead on the way back to the dorm so Ian and I could be alone for the last time. I was determined not to cry again. Twice in twenty-four hours was over my limit.

We were walking hand in hand up the path through the Haunted Forest, neither of us knowing what to say. I wanted to tell Ian that I really, really liked him, that he was the best thing to have come into my life, ever, but it seemed ridiculous, considering that we'd just gotten together and we'd probably never see each other again.

Finally, Ian stopped right before we entered Fiddler's Green. "Look. I want to say something."

"Me too."

He sighed. "Okay, that's it. That's all I came up with."

"That you wanted to say something?" I laughed. "The entire summer you can't shut up with your bad puns, and suddenly you're speechless?"

He ran his finger along my chin. "That's what happens when all that's left is good-bye." He cringed. "That sounds like a bad Sage Adams lyric, doesn't it?"

"I've got news for you. All of Sage Adams's lyrics are bad."

"God, you're great." Ian bent down and kissed me slowly and softly. It was the kind of kiss you give someone when you're pretty sure you'll never see them again and you want to leave a lasting impression.

He hooked his arms around my neck. "I don't want you to go."

Understatement of the year. "If you're ever back in Jersey . . ." I began.

"Oh, I'll be back in Jersey. Didn't I tell you? I'm moving in with you for senior year. I hope that's not a problem, you know, now that I've *seen your eye tis.*"

Senioritis. "That pun is a fail on so many levels. I mean, the last part makes no sense."

"It would if I were with a bunch of guys."

I forced a smile. "Just don't say this is the end, okay? Just say we'll keep in touch and maybe run into each other, you know, in the near future."

"Zoe." Ian did his dead-serious thing. "You don't understand. Nothing is going to keep me away from you, certainly not three thousand wimpy miles and definitely not the Queen. Don't sell me short." He gave me one last kiss. "It's not over by a long shot."

Because Jess is Jess, she insisted on spending the night with me in her old bed. I kept the mood light by going over all the crazy things that had happened at Fairyland, like my first and last performance as Cinderella and the time the Queen thought she had been blinded by a dust mote and Tinker Bell's attempts to do me in.

We'd barely fallen asleep, it seemed, when the alarm rang. My last early morning to walk Tink, and even that chore was bittersweet. I let Jess snooze as I slipped into my shorts and hoodie, wrapped my hair in a band, grabbed my bag, and headed out into the park.

Now that it was mid-August, dawn came later, around six o'clock in the morning, for which I was extremely grateful as I trudged through an autumnal mist over the dew-soaked grass. I let myself into Tinker Bell's boudoir, roused her out of bed, and snapped on her collar. Tricking myself into believing that this was any other morning and that I would be back doing the same thing tomorrow, I led her around her favorite bush, waving to the Maintenance guys inspecting the benches for gum and the gardeners searching for weeds among the petunias.

When I returned I found the Queen waiting in full regalia, arms crossed.

"I was prepared to exercise Precious myself," she said. "As I must do tomorrow."

I sadly hung up the leash.

The Queen flung out her hand. "ID, master key, and telephonic device. We might as well get this over with now."

"Here?" I was expecting a more formal exit in her office. Not in the doghouse. Literally.

"Here."

I reached into my bag, got my ID, and placed it in her hand along with the master key and iPhone. "That's it. Can I go?"

"Hmm." The Queen set aside my ID and master key, but, as I'd feared, she searched my phone.

"I thought so." She frowned and flipped the phone around to show me RJ's number. "Do you know what this is?"

"It's RJ's number. On speed dial." I mean, really, what did I have to lose? I was already history.

"What's RJ doing with a cell phone?"

I was tempted to tell her the truth. But then I realized that RJ was acting with good intentions. He was trying to save the Pinelands and the endangered amphibians and the spike-nosed whatnot, so I wasn't about to turn him in for that. No reason both of us had to lose our jobs.

"I have no idea, ma'am. But I can assure you that I never called him." *Or gave him the progress report.*

"Then I will simply ask him himself."

I braced for the worst as she pressed his number and put the phone to her ear. "No, RJ," she snapped. "This is not Zoe. This is your boss."

Crap!

There was some frantic mumbling on his end. The Queen straightened her posture, clearly not buying whatever excuse he'd invented.

"You have precisely five minutes to be out of bed and presentable," she said. "A security patrol officer will escort you to my office, where I will hold an official inquiry. Don't be tardy."

Oh, god. This was going to be bad.

She slid the phone to Off and then unhooked the radio from her belt, the radio she used only to call the trolls. Speaking into it, she said, "I need you to bring RJ to my office posthaste. Also secure the perimeter and make sure no one exits or egresses until I give the command."

Lifting her finger from the button of the radio, she

turned to me with a sly smile. "Very good, Zoe. You have managed to trap our spy."

Spy?

But Ian had been the spy—or, to be more accurate, the one who'd been crossing into the Forbidden Zone—and before that, Marcus.

Poor, innocent Marcus.

I rushed to keep up with her as the Queen sailed down the hall to her office, brimming with power. Two trolls on alert outside her door parted to let her in. The door slid open, and there, chilling with Andy over a couple of cups of coffee, was RJ wearing a huge grin.

The door slid closed, and the three of them erupted into enthusiastic applause.

"Brilliant!" The Queen clapped madly. "Simply brilliant, Zoe. With that kind of Wow! spirit, I knew you'd win."

"What?" I said. "What did I win?"

The Queen placed her skeletal fingers on my shoulder and pushed me into a chair. "Why, the Dream and Do, my dear."

But . . . but that was impossible. I was supposed to be on the bus back to Bridgewater in just a few hours. I'd been *fired*!

Andy raised his hand. "I'll confess. I didn't think she could do it."

"I know, right?" RJ chimed in. "When I was laying it on her, I kept thinking this is crazy. It's too much. How's this girl expected to turn down fifty grand *and* a chance to save the environment?"

"The spike-nosed hornbeam turtle." The Queen erupted into a full-throated laugh, even pinching her nose to stop. "I mean, honestly, RJ. Where *did* you come up with that?"

RJ threw up his hands. "Beats me. Discovery Channel? I dunno."

I had no idea what was going on. Had my firing and RJ's bribe been lies? Or was this more of their cruelty?

"Wait," I said. "Is Fairyland building another theme park or not?"

The Queen dabbed her eyes with a doily. "Oh, there was a PUD:1,001 once upon a time. But that project was jettisoned years ago for environmental reasons. Since then we've been using those files for the Final Exam, which you passed with flying colors when you decided against giving RJ the progress report. Brava!"

I glanced from RJ to the Queen to Andy, who was busily helping himself to coffee and breakfast laid out on the side table. "In other words sending me to get the PUD:1,001 report had been a setup."

The Queen said, "We prefer to think of it as a test."

"A test?" None of this was rational. "What for?"

"To win the Dream and Do, silly." Andy shook his head. "Seriously, Zoe, are you just caffeine-deprived? You took the test. You passed. And now you'll win the Dream and Do. In other words you are now twenty-five thousand dollars richer."

They were messing with my mind. "I couldn't have won the grant. I did so many things wrong." There had to be a mistake. My litany of grievances was huge. "I picked flowers and crossed into the Forbidden Zone."

"Twice, I might add." The Queen nudged RJ. "You remember the quicksand? Oh, dear lord, I was on the verge of sending the trolls out there myself if Ian hadn't happened along."

RJ nodded. "That was dicey. I was a little worried, too."

"Don't forget her confrontation with Jake the Hansel," Andy added. "I thought Jake was about to lose it for a minute there, and I must admit that staying in costume was a particularly delightful touch."

"That reminds me." The Queen grabbed her cell, the one she'd loaned me, and rapidly texted like a teenager. "I need to put something extra in Jake's final stipend check. He did a superb job."

"He's going to be *very* disappointed when he finds out he didn't win the grant," RJ said.

The Queen lifted a shoulder nonchalantly. "He'll live.

Now come here, Zoe, I want to give you a hug."

I went stiff as her bony arms awkwardly wrapped around me. "Do you know why I picked you to be my assistant, Zoe? Because, as a young girl, I'd also lost my mother, and I knew when I read your essay about Storytown that you not only had the potential to meet my highest expectations, but that without a maternal figure you were desperately in need of nurturing female guidance."

Now I was the one laughing, since *nurturing* was not the word I would have associated with a woman who sent me into the dark woods at midnight to fetch a sleeping potion she hadn't needed. "Thank you, ma'am. . . ."

"Helen," she clarified, clasping me tighter. "Helen Reynolds McNeil."

HRM. It said so right outside her door, though I'd assumed the initials had stood for Her Royal Majesty.

"Ma'am," I said, unable to break the habit. "I mean Helen. What about Marcus?"

She twirled me around so we were face-to-face. "Listen, don't you worry about Marcus. He was a disaster from the get-go and sent home in the interests of his own safety. That boy was destined to break his back, but, if you're still unsure, you should know that I received an email that he's surfing and doing fine."

"And Dash? And Valerie? Were they in on the joke, too?"

After all, Dash had snagged Jake the Hansel's report from the Box of Whine. Had he been trying to earn my trust by stealing Jake's letter? Or maybe I'd been wrong about that, too.

At the mention of Dash and Valerie, the Queen allowed a glimpse of her chilly former self. "No." Her tone was clipped. "I've made it a policy not to discuss the performance of current cast members, but perhaps it will help if I explain something."

She sat me down and perched herself on the desk. "This internship serves a dual purpose. Providing rising high school seniors with experience acting in the park is one, but it is not the primary reason Fairyland runs the program. The internship is the best way for us to identify young talent who will go on to become loyal and dedicated team players as Fairyland executives, either here or in the parent company in Düsseldorf."

Andy and RJ nodded in agreement. "Helen's right," RJ said. "Almost all the executives at Fairyland are former interns. That's why we take the Game and, especially, the Final Exam very seriously."

The Queen said, "As a result we enjoy working here because—aside from a fantastic benefits package, including an impressive retirement savings plan—we know that we're more than employees. We consider ourselves members of the Fairyland family, with all the support and encouragement commonly found in such societal groups. I'm afraid that in the case of some interns . . ."

Meaning Dash and Valerie.

". . . the competitive spirit eclipsed that bonhomie, and they allowed their personal ambitions to surpass their moral underpinnings for a truly Machiavellian dynamic of the ends justifying the means."

She might have been slightly nicer, but with that SAT vocabulary she was still the Queen.

"I think I get it," I said. "Undercutting isn't really showing that Wow! spirit."

The Queen rewarded me with a pat. "You showed that Wow! spirit by putting yourself last, Zoe, and your cousin Jess and Fairyland first. You could have turned over the progress report to RJ—heck, I would have been tempted to myself, after his bleeding-heart speech—but you didn't, because you consider yourself a member of our family, and you know what we say in Fairyland?"

"The slipper always fits?"

"Exactly." She held out her hand. "Now where is that progress report?"

I was reaching into my bag to get it when a noisy scuffle erupted in the hall. The door slid open, and Michelle— Sage's mother/manager—burst in, her red corkscrew curls flying in every direction. "You lost my son! He didn't come home last night, and he's still missing!"

I slapped my cheek, alarmed. Sage hadn't returned, and that would be the end to all this bon vivant, bonhomie, bon-whatever stuff. The one thing I wasn't supposed to do—take Sage to Storytown—and I'd bombed that, big-time.

"Forget it, Mickey," the Queen said with a wave. "Zoe knows."

Michelle blinked. "Oh, shoot. I'm too late." She placed her hands on her hips. "Boy, that was fun. I hope you'll let me do it again."

The Queen handed her a cup of coffee. "You have to be the bitchiest stage mother ever."

"Coming from you, that is high praise." Michelle or Mickey or whoever gave me a wink.

"Even you and Sage were part of the exam?" I asked. "How did that happen?"

Michelle placed her cup in its saucer. "When we were negotiating the spokesperson deal this spring, Helen told us about the Game and the Final Exam, and Sage insisted on playing a part. We had to rearrange his schedule to squeeze this in, but he was adamant."

I thought about this. "He was adamant about being part of my Final Exam?"

The Queen bit into a cheese Danish, wiped her mouth, and said, "Not *your* Final Exam, my dear. *Ian's.*"

* * *

I watched the monitor on which the Queen, back in character, and Andy and Michelle stood on the stage outside the Princess Palace waiting for the trolls to haul Sage and Ian from Storytown.

Enough of the initial shock had worn off, so that I had calmed down and was beginning to enjoy myself, though you might say I was waiting for the other glass slipper to drop. I was sure the Queen would say I'd really been fired and that the Game and the Final Exam had all been pranks.

What bothered me were the princesses. They'd been weighed nearly every day to make sure they had stayed the same sizes. When I'd mentioned the sexism of that to the Queen, she'd brushed it off with some statement about corporate policy being set in stone. Personally that didn't seem very "family-friendly" to me. Then again it was my understanding that the Mouse did the same with its princesses, so perhaps this was standard for fairy-tale theme parks. Didn't make it right, though.

"How do you think Ian's going to react when he finds out Sage intentionally kissed you just to get him mad?" RJ asked. "Should I have my fists up in case he takes a swing at the nearest male?"

I gave him a look. "Ian's not like that. And you people did provoke him, admit it."

RJ went back to the monitor. "Yeah, well, he was

supposed to lash out at Sage, not Dash. That turned out to be an added bonus."

I now knew that RJ really didn't like the guy, and I couldn't blame him. Apparently Dash had been filing regular mini reports in the Box of Whine ratting on each of us, including RJ for hooking up with Jess (a violation of Fairyland Rule #103). But Dash hadn't acted alone.

Much to my shock, Valerie had been scheming with him, too.

That's how Dash learned I'd been in the Forbidden Zone and that I knew Marcus wasn't the real spy. It had been Valerie who'd been in the bathroom eavesdropping on my discussion with Jess. And she ran right back to tell her boyfriend, so they could trash our reputations with the Queen.

I watched monitor #22. "So Ian and I will be the only ones who know?"

"Yup. Otherwise, even with all the confidentiality agreements you interns sign, it would get out, and the Game would be ruined." RJ swiveled to inspect monitor #19, the one in the Haunted Forest, where a group of figures were gradually coming from the shadows. "You and Ian will keep it a secret, because you'll have an incentive."

Incentive?

Was that Adele? I moved closer to the screen. "What's she doing with Ian and Sage?"

The trolls were bringing the three scofflaws to the Queen, who greeted them with her royal disapproval. Michelle looked like she was throwing a hysterical fit, ranting and raving about the outrage of it all. Andy pretended to act anxious, wringing his hands and pacing. Now they were being led to the office, Ian with his head down and Adele trying really hard not to smile

RJ pumped his fist. "Adele's awesome, isn't she? It was her idea to play a temperamental princess who runs off to hide out in Storytown. And being away from the park gave her a chance to work in the off-site studio recording new songs and dances for the parade. That's her major at Barnard, you know, music."

I didn't, of course. Up until two seconds ago, I'd thought she was a farm girl from Wisconsin. "So you and Adele . . ."

"Won the Dream and Do last year, just like you and Ian are going to win it this year. And then, come next summer, you two will return to the park as RAs to train a whole new set of interns."

The door slid open, and the group stumbled in. Ian took one look at me hanging out with RJ and with a booming Texan shout exclaimed, "I *knew* it!"

Ian would later claim that, from the get-go, he'd suspected something was up. As proof, he noted that the Queen did not flip out when he confessed that he'd been the one in the Forbidden Zone so Marcus wouldn't be unfairly sent home to California, an act of selflessness that Her Majesty considered the ultimate example of Wow!™ spirit.

"Obviously it was some sort of test," he said. "I have a sixth sense about these things. Legit."

My response to him was, "Oh, yeah? Then if you were so convinced this was a game, then why did you go to Storytown after saying good-bye to me last night to convince Sage that he should sign the contract to be a spokesman so I'd get my job back?"

"CYA, Zoe. Pure Cover Your Ass."

I had my doubts. Anyway, by returning to Storytown and begging Sage to ask his mother to reconsider canceling the deal, Ian had passed the Final Exam and won the boys' Dream & Do. So, as they say in Fairyland, All's Well That Ends Well and It Always Ends Well.

The most difficult part, actually, was that Ian and I couldn't tell anyone about the Game, not even Jess, which was ridiculous since Jess and I shared everything. Worse, she kept saying how bad she felt that I'd been treated so unfairly and how she was going to do something to set things right.

She even went to the Queen to plead my case, and the Queen had snapped that Jess had overstepped her position and that whatever happened to me was none of her business. Then she ordered Jess to work a double shift as punishment for her insolence.

Broke my heart.

For seven whole days until the Dream & Do ceremony, I had to go around pretending that the only reason I'd been allowed to stay until the end of the internship was because the Queen didn't want to cover a sixty-dollar bus ticket to send me back to Bridgewater.

Every morning I walked Tinker Bell and dressed in my dove-gray gown and brought my boss her tray of newspapers and tiny food as if nothing had changed. At night Ian and I would sneak off to swim at the old gristmill and make out on the beach under the stars. When we weren't kissing—and we did *a lot* of kissing—we would lie back on the sand and plan the next summer. Everything was perfect, except for one major glitch that I needed to fix ASAP.

On my second-to-last day at Fairyland, I summoned my nerve to take the Queen aside. "I have something to ask you," I said, anxious not to appear disgraceful in any way. "It has to do with the Dream and Do—"

She stopped me. "I know what you're going to say, Zoe. I had the feeling you might change your mind. That's why we want you to be part of the Fairyland family."

It will always be a highlight of my life when the two winners were announced and Jess, crying and laughing for joy, gave me a huge hug. "You did it, Zoe."

"*You* did it," I said, hugging her right back. "Now, quick, you'd better get up there before Valerie climbs over everyone and grabs your money."

With one last smile of gratitude, Jess took her spot next to Ian, who gave me a thumbs-up, even though only a half hour before he'd told me that turning down the grant, while kind and sacrificial and all that, was just plain stupid.

"It's not like you don't need the money, too, you know," he'd said when we'd managed to steal a minute alone. "What about your mom's leftover medical bills and *your* college tuition?"

I knew what really had him worried: that because I hadn't won the Dream & Do, I wouldn't join him here next summer to corral a new herd of interns, and I thought that was really sweet.

"Got it covered," I'd said, slipping my arms around his neck and pressing his nose to mine. "Since Jess doesn't know how all this works, she doesn't expect to come back. It'll be you and me next June, Ian, so be good until then."

He'd grinned. "But it's so much more fun being bad." And then he'd kissed me in a way that was absolutely wicked.

That's what I was thinking about—kissing Ian and how great next summer would be—as the Queen presented the twenty-five-thousand-dollar checks and awards. After-ward she gave a speech praising Ian's upbeat attitude, his excellence as Puss 'n Boots, his willingness to help "a certain prince" learn how to ride horses on his off-hours, his stellar performance as Prince Charming, and, finally, "going above and beyond" to insure that Sage Adams signed on as the Fairyland spokesman—which was a little white lie, since Sage had already signed, but whatever.

Turning to Jess, the Queen applauded the "indomitable Wow! spirit" Jess displayed in her gripping portrayal of Red Riding Hood and, later, as Cinderella, a role she embraced with "unprecedented enthusiasm," working both the morning breakfasts and tuck-in services at the resort, always cheerfully and willingly, never a complaint.

"Last," the Queen said, zeroing in on me, "there is an unsung heroine here who gave of herself so willingly that she insisted I not publicly afford her credit. This girl requires no Dream and Do grant, because she is already a doer who, I am certain, is fully capable of making all her dreams come true."

Well, maybe not *all* my dreams, I thought, smiling to Ian, who was smiling back. But most. Which was fine, since I'd learned that getting *most* of what you wish for in life is often just as good as getting it all.

Turn the page for a sneak peek at Sarah Strohmeyer's

SMART GIRLS GET WHAT THEY WANT

I've decided Halloween when you're sixteen pretty much epitomizes the concept of adolescent purgatory.

On the one hand, the kid in you can't believe the days of harassing neighbors for sugar loot have swiftly come to an end. And yet, the prospect of beating aside four-year-olds for the last Giant Pixy Stix on the block seems somehow wrong.

For years, Neerja, Bea, and I have managed to deal with this moral dilemma by getting together to watch *The Blair Witch Project,* which is good for a laugh because inevitably Bea, hopped up on a mega-mix bag of Tootsie Rolls and Starbursts, will yell, "Follow the river. Follow the river, you idiots. Seriously, just how stupid are you?"

I'd so miss that this year.

This year, because Halloween fell on a Saturday, the day before her brother's birthday, Bea's parents were taking her and George out to dinner at Legal Sea Foods. I'm sure this is exactly how Bea's brother wants to celebrate the big two-oh, by listening to his father bicker with a waitress over the price of oysters instead of going with his friends to a Halloween party on campus. But, when you're Harry Honeycutt's kid, you tend not to disagree.

Neerja, meanwhile, was stuck babysitting The Things while her parents, attired in matching clown suits, attempted to cheer up/frighten to death Dr. Padwami's elderly patients. After that, the whole Padwami clan was off to a party of doctors—which left me to celebrate Halloween alone, with Marmie.

Anyway, with nothing much to do, I was updating my status on Facebook from "in a relationship with Petunia Dubois" to "it's complicated," when Mike's chat screen appeared at the bottom of my page.

Mike: U going to Ava's party?

I thought, *Ava's having a party and she didn't invite me?*

Me: Nope
Mike: Aren't u 2 friends?

Me: Guess not
Mike: U can come w/us

Right. Just what I wanted, to tag behind Mike and his equally tall and beautiful girlfriend, Sienna, as the slightly irregular but intelligent third wheel? Um, pass. Though it was thoughtful of him to ask, I'd give him that.

Me: Thanks, but I have plans
Mike: OK. Bye!

I logged off and lay on my bed, staring at my ceiling as I fought an existential crisis.

See, this is the problem with Facebook. If I hadn't gone on, I would have remained blissfully ignorant about Ava's party. I might even have had fun by myself knitting the scarf I was making my mother for Christmas and watching *Blair Witch* and teasing the cute trick-or-treaters. But now, I couldn't shake the insult of total rejection.

Ava and I might not have been as close as before her Rolf days, but at least she could have included me in her first-ever Halloween party. Apparently Mike thought so too, otherwise he wouldn't have asked me so casually *Aren't u 2 friends?*

Exactly.

The doorbell rang again, sending Petunia into a crazy

tailspin of barking and baying at the latest round of trick-or-treaters. It was the Brezinski brothers dressed up as ninja warriors/pirates/*Star Wars* Stormtroopers. They lived three doors down and their front yard was dirt from all the damage they'd inflicted on the grass by digging, scraping, and wrestling like maniacs.

I held out the bowl of candy and they whined in unison, "Not Reese's Peanut Butter Cups. EVERYONE gives out those."

All righty then. I put the bowl back on the table, crossed my arms, and said, "Trick."

Stuart Brezinski, the youngest of the gang at about age six, said, "What do you mean, trick?"

"It's trick-or-treat, right? So you guys have to do some tricks 'cause you dissed my treats."

The oldest, Marcus, gave him a light punch. "Come on, Stewy. Let's go."

But Stuart was intrigued. "Like magic tricks?"

"Like egging her house," his other brother, Andrew, said. "Toilet-papering her car."

"I dare you."

Their faces lit up. Even under their masks, you could tell their greedy eyes were shining with delight at the prospect of actually being encouraged to commit minor acts of vandalism. Now, *this* was Halloween!

They hopped off our front steps and ran down the

walk, heads bent together. I had to laugh at their evil glee. What a bunch of little thugs.

"That's a bit dangerous, don't you think?"

I hadn't even noticed Will standing there in a red-lined black satin cape, hands in jeans pockets. I'm not a diehard vamp fan, but IMHO guys should wear capes 24/7. With his jet-black hair, he looked like an Edward Cullen fantasy come to life.

"Don't you think you're a little old to be begging for candy?" I said, my blood suddenly pulsing as I remembered his comment on Mike's Facebook page. "Or is this how they do things in California?"

"This is how they do things in Massachusetts when you have a seven-year-old brother who's new to the neighborhood." He nodded to his left, where a vampire in miniature was skipping toward him down the sidewalk. "I'm waiting at the end of the street to give him a sense of 'independence,'" he said, making air quotes around the word.

I couldn't help but be touched. I also couldn't help but wonder if he'd been invited to Ava's party too. Bet he had. "That's very sweet."

"That's what big brothers are for. By the way, I forgot to ask Mike. How did it go with Schultz?"

"We were acquitted. That's the good news. The bad news is we have to do a project together and we still get letters in our permanent files saying we were referred to the principal for cheating."

He made a face. "That's not right."

"Word."

The miniature vampire came to a skipping halt and, after flashing me a questioning glance, tugged on Will's cape. Will kneeled down and let him whisper into his ear. This was too darned cute.

"Ah," Will said, smiling. "So my man Aidan here"— he ruffled his brother's hair—"would like to know if he could use, um, your facilities."

It took me a second to define facilities. But then I got it. "Oh! No problem."

I waved them inside, trying to remember if I'd removed the spare emergency Tampax from its place of honor on the top of the toilet tank. I'm kind of lazy about leaving that stuff around, seeing as we don't get much call for menfolk in these here parts.

"But you have to be careful," I said to Aidan. "There's a killer basset inside."

Petunia howled and Aidan shrank into Will.

"She's kidding." Though Will himself didn't seem so certain. "Right?"

Petunia howled again. "You'll just have to take your chances."

Aidan seemed pretty scared when he went through the vestibule into the house, until he saw my fat, elongated, stub-legged dog, a mass of wiggles and wags, so incredibly overjoyed to see a real live kid approaching her with a bag of chocolate that she was drooling.

"Bayooooo!" Petunia bayed happily as Aidan shyly extended a hand to pet her pointed head.

I took his candy bag and placed it high on the bookshelf out of her reach. If dogs could curse, Petunia would have rattled off a blue streak.

Will leaned down to pet her. "What is this thing? It almost looks like a dog, and yet it's totally distorted."

"That, my good man, is an eating machine. Hamburgers. Cookies. Entire chickens. Spare auto parts. Doesn't matter, she'll eat it, especially if it's coated in sugar." I gave her a kiss. She smelled like corn chips.

"Her ears are long." You could tell Aidan was dying to touch one.

"And soft. Go ahead. She loves to have her ears stroked."

He did so gently. "Why come they're so long?"

"Supposedly, so she can sweep more smell toward her nose. But really it's so she'll be able to collect the last bits of food from her bowl." And I showed him how Petunia could easily suck on their ends.

Aidan chortled. "I want a dog like this."

Petunia bayed in approval.

Will said, "I thought you wanted to use the bathroom."

"Oh, yeah, right." And hopping up, Aidan followed my directions to the end of the hall.

"Close the door!" Will yelled. Then, as way of explanation, said, "We live in a house of men."

"Oddly enough, I live in a house of only women. My grandmother, mother, and me."

He smiled, his teeth a blazing white. Which was when it hit me that this guy, who was by far the hottest member of the male species I'd ever seen off a screen—J.Crew looks, square jaw, gorgeous bone structure, and those eyes—was also standing in our kitchen, where I frequently whipped up my disgusting creations, like pizza-bagel egg sandwiches with hot sauce and salsa.

"Can I get you anything?"

"Nah, thanks. I snuck some of Aidan's candy." His gaze drifted to Marmie's half-open bottle of wine and leftover cheese and bread from dinner. "So, where's your father?"

Adults cringe when they hear this question because they feel sorry for me, the half-orphaned child. But having known nothing but a brilliant absentee dad with zero directional sense, it's really no big deal. I find it kind of funny.

"My parents broke up before I was born, though since they're both scientists, I've long held suspicions that I'm indeed an alien."

Will laughed.

I said, "And your tale of woe?"

"Mom's in L.A."

"Oh. Okay." Kind of odd. "Permanently?"

He stroked Petunia under her flabby chin. "We don't know. My parents separated last year when Dad got this offer to teach at Tufts. Mom didn't want to shut down her interior decorating business in California and Dad wanted to return to the East Coast, so we're doing a test run. Can the three Blake men survive on their own?"

Already I had a million questions. Why didn't he and Aidan stay with their mother, for starters. But I didn't think it right to ask, considering we'd talked maybe twice.

Will stood, shook Petunia hair off his cape, and lowered his voice. "Aidan doesn't know this, but actually it was Mom who wanted the break. From *us*."

Geesh. That was harsh. I mean, my mother also lived thousands of miles away, but that was because she worked as an internationally renowned nerd, not because she was in need of some "me" time. "I'm sorry."

"That's L.A. It does weird things to people sometimes. Dad and I are hoping that she'll snap out of it."

The toilet flushed and I decided it might be wise to change the subject. "And how's Aidan liking Boston?"

"So-so. He really misses our home and his buddies. He hasn't been sleeping in his own bed since we got here, so he's been sleeping with me."

A vision of Will Blake in bed popped into my head and I blushed, rushing back to the safe, neutral subject of his brother. "Is that a good thing or a bad thing?"

"Mostly a bad thing. He kicks constantly and tends to wake up with the sun. Then he drags me out of bed to watch cartoons. I'm seriously sleep-deprived."

I could not be held accountable for my actions if someone dragged me out of my bed at dawn to watch cartoons. "May I just be so bold as to say that sucks?"

"You may. But if sleeping with me helps Aidan adjust, then it's worth it. That's one reason why I'm going to Denton instead of a boarding school—so I can be here for him. That said, I'm majorly bumming about leaving L.A. and . . ."

Here comes the part where he mentions a hot girl-friend.

". . . anyway, it's kind of weird going to a school where you don't know anyone and you're used to being in a place where it's always sunny and warm and you've got tons of friends. It's a serious culture shock."

"I bet." *And the girlfriend . . . ?*

"I'm trying to get psyched about being here. I know Boston's an awesome city with lots of history and funky hangouts and—"

"Let me give you a tour!" I had no idea where that

came from. I'm not normally in the habit of boldly asking out strange boys. Okay, to be technically correct, *any* boys. It's just that Will really got me with the story about his mother, and Aidan not sleeping. Or, maybe, Will really got me with his blue eyes and that sexy jaw. "I'd be happy to show you around."

"For real?" He looked taken aback, and I remembered what Henry said about Lindsay, how it's awkward to ask out someone you hardly hang with. "Well, you know . . ."

Fortunately, the powder room door opened and there was a brief sound of water being turned off and on as my hero Aidan emerged to save my self-respect. "I'm done!" he boasted.

"We can take Aidan to the science museum and the aquarium!" I slapped my thigh like this was *exactly* what I'd had in mind. "Has he ever seen a seal before?"

"We, uh, lived in California."

Moron. "Okay, then a lobster. I bet he's never seen a live New England lobster."

"Restaurants? You know those tanks?" He wiggled his fingers to imitate lobster crawling.

"I've never seen a moray eel except on The Discovery Channel," Aidan said. "They're mega poisonous."

"*Wicked*," I corrected. "Now that you're in Massachusetts, young man, your preferred hyperbolic adjective is 'wicked.' As in, Petunia is a wicked fat dog. Or, Gigi, you're a wicked gorgeous creature."

Aidan gamely played along. "Moray eels are wicked poisonous."

"Atta boy. Actually the moray isn't that bad, though all eel blood is poisonous to humans—a fact that won Charles Richet a Nobel Prize for determining that you could die from an allergic reaction to a toxic substance. Isn't that fascinating?"

Aidan was blunt. "Not really."

Ah, the refreshing honesty of youth. I switched tacks. "However, if you want to see something really cool, there's a thirty-foot octopus named Truman in the aquarium's center tank."

"*Awesome!*" Aidan clapped. "I love octopi. Do they have blue-ringed? Those are my favorite."

"I don't know. We'll have to see."

Will gave Aidan a slight push toward the door. "Great. I'll text you and we can work it out. Weekends are kind of"—he nodded in the direction of Aidan, who was on tiptoe, trying to reach the bag of candy—"hard."

"Gotcha." I fetched the bag and hooked my finger around Petunia's collar so she couldn't follow them home. Aidan toddled out the door and Will hung back, letting him go. Taking my elbow, he looked deep into my eyes and said, "Thanks. That was really nice of you. Means a lot."

I got all warm, though I tried to act like it was nothing. "Sure. It'll be fun."

"For me, too." He smiled and then jogged to catch Aidan from crossing the street alone. They waved goodbye and turned the corner as I shut the door and realized something. Now I knew why Halloween takes a backseat as you grow up, because there are so many sweeter things to look forward to than Snickers bars.

Like Will.

Not so much that giant octopus.